Praise for Stine Pilgaard

"Pilgaard has the formidable ability to give a new twist to language and fixed expressions."
Litteratursiden

"Pilgaard has a great sense for the ironic twist hiding in any situation."
Dagbladet Information

•

Praise for My Mother Says

"With undying optimism and a sting of melancholy, Stine Pilgaard portrays the frailty of conversation in this hilarious queer break-up story. Nobody writes dialogue like Pilgaard. Her musicality gets you first, then you stay for the warmth and the acceptance of loneliness as a condition of life. Few books make me laugh out loud as much as this one. This wise writer is one of Denmark's most beloved authors."
OLGA RAVN, author of *The Employees*

"Stine Pilgaard's debut whirls with elegance and energy."
Politiken

"A novel about getting over a broken heart without drowning in self-pity, but also a novel about language and communication, dialogue versus monologue, and community versus loneliness."
Stavanger Aftenblad

"A pearl of linguistic abundance. ... Stine Pilgaard's debut novel is an original, humorous, and slightly absurd universe of misunderstandings. The narrator's affection for the characters turns the humor into loving comedy."
Litteratursiden

"An incredibly promising and slyly hilarious debut novel. ... Pilgaard writes bravely, without hesitation, and with a sarcasm and subtle humor that shines through the book's many conversations, and invites the reader into an affectionate and joyful relationship with the characters."
Fyens Stifstidende

"Stine Pilgaard has written this winter's must-read. ... It's an impressive debut, I'm going to read it again right away."
Weekendavisen

"With its references to the psalms of the baroque, *My Mother Says* is both highly literary and deeply communicative. This is a novel that reaches out to its reader, and it does so by being uncommonly entertaining."
Information

"Stine Pilgaard is a debut author you should get to know. *My Mother Says* is breezy and full of humor. I caught myself laughing out loud several times, even though the novel is about the pain of a broken heart."
Femina

"An exuberant debut novel."
Extra Bladet

Praise for The Land of Short Sentences

"Small communities love their inside jokes, which become all the more (and paradoxically) hilarious if an outsider takes them seriously. Pilgaard's smart, layered parody will make you laugh without knowing exactly why, and then will keep you laughing at your self-consciousness."
VERONICA RAIMO, author of *The Girl at the Door*

"A charming and funny novel. ... The buzz of people coming and going through the pages, and the warmth and wit of the narrator's voice, make it a pleasure to be in her company."
The Guardian

"Stine Pilgaard's novel is a charming chamber work, focusing on a handful of characters in a relatively isolated location, from the perspective of a protagonist struggling to find her own place in society. Her advice columns make for a fascinating contrast with the stories of her life, and a few unlikely narrative payoffs make these seemingly distanced aspects more connected than you'd expect."
Words Without Borders

"A different and refreshing novel. It's wise, funny and sad by turns and has a powerful sense of place."
Daily Mail

"A gentle observational comedy. ... Pilgaard draws out a great deal of warmth and humour from the narrator's attempts to connect with the locals."
The Herald

"Hunter Simpson's translation is playful, funny, and colorful without being showy, rendering the world of a Folk High School in West Jutland with warmth and precision and the voice of the novel's witty fish-out-of-water narrator with panache."
Jury, Leif and Inger Sjöberg Prize for Translation, 2021

"A master of irony lays down her weapons. A deliciously crumbly novel oozing with awkward love."
Weekendavisen

"A sheer delight: Stine Pilgaard has penned a perfect comedy about normalcy."
Dagbladet Information

"*The Land of Short Sentences* comfortably won the Golden Laurels award, receiving over half the votes of Denmark's bookstores. ... The book of the year. An absolutely fabulous novel about adjusting to midlife in the back of beyond."
Jyllands-Posten

"Stine Pilgaard has a pronounced talent for parody. She can write in such a way as to make you laugh out loud, bringing our embarrassments out into the open, capturing the absurdities of everyday life. Her dialogues are natural and precise, her language clear and succinct, and her references plain and recognizable.

But beneath the lightness of her prose hides something beyond comedy and rhetoric."
Berlingske

"Another Pilgaard pearl. Too funny for words and at the same time so keenly intelligent in its depictions. You love her characters to bits and understand their faltering steps on the road to community so well. A book you'll cherish reading—again and again and ..."
SØNDAG

"Stine Pilgaard's crisp prose and supreme timing can be spotted fifty books away. It's an exquisite pearl of a book, wonderfully funny, playful, and subtle in its crafting. But don't be mistaken: beneath the humor there's a worldly-wise voice with a finely honed ability to put into words all that's profound and beautiful and good about life. This is one of the best works of Danish literature I've read in ages."
Litteratursiden

"*The Land of Short Sentences* is a tragicomic genre hybrid including advice columns, *højskole* songs, and a thoroughly maladapted, infinitely charming narrator. The book's disasters are small, and it is a situational comedy that gives us a break from world events. But it is not cozily escapist or trivial; it is a consolation, a reminder of something common, comical, and troublesome that persists while dramatic global events take place: the fact that people need people, no matter how awkward it can be. Dear Stine Pilgaard. I would like to say congratulations on the award, but also: thank you for the book. Because it made it a little

easier to live, without lying about it being easy. Because it lingered with irresistible joy on all the little inconveniences that make up the social landscape. Because it made it much easier to be a weirdo who ventures across the boundaries of others with the best of intentions."
LINEA MAJA ERNST, *Weekendavisen*

"Pilgaard has written an entertaining parody of the rural idyll. With dry Danish humor she describes the difficult integration of a woman in West Jutland. The problems that men and women of all ages spew into the letter section are all too recognizable. Divorces, alcoholism, jealousy and work addiction, everything is discussed."
De Volkskrant

"What an absolutely wonderful book."
Het Parool

"Pilgaard is one of the most talented writers in Denmark. In the mildly satirical *The Land of Short Sentences*, she provides both entertainment and depth. The book is a sharp diagnosis of Scandinavian modern-family resentment and of outrageous idealism and social alienation."
De Morgen

My Mother Says

STINE PILGAARD

My Mother Says

Translated from the Danish
by Hunter Simpson

WORLD EDITIONS
New York, London, Amsterdam

Published in the USA in 2023 by World Editions LLC, New York
Published in the UK in 2023 by World Editions Ltd., London

World Editions
New York/London/Amsterdam

Min mor siger © Stine Pilgaard and Samleren/ROSINANTE&Co, København, 2012
Published by agreement with Winje Agency A/S, Norway
English translation copyright © Hunter Simpson, 2023
Cover illustration © Annemarie van Haeringen
Author portrait © Alexander Banck-Petersen

Printed by Zwaan Lenoir, NL
World Editions is committed to a sustainable future. Papers used by World Editions meet the PEFC standards of certification.

This book is a work of fiction. Any resemblance to actual persons, living or dead, or actual events is purely coincidental.

British Library Cataloguing-in-Publication Data. A catalogue record for this book is available on request from the British Library.

ISBN 978-1-912987-52-8

First published as *Min mor siger* in Denmark in 2012 by Samleren, Copenhagen

This publication has been made possible with financial support from the Danish Arts Foundation

Danish Arts Foundation

All rights reserved. No part of this publication may be reproduced, stored in or introduced into a retrieval system, or transmitted, in any form, or by any means (electronic, mechanical, photocopying, recording or otherwise) without the prior written permission of the publisher.

Company: worldeditions.org
Facebook: @WorldEditionsInternationalPublishing
Instagram: @WorldEdBooks
TikTok: @worldeditions_tok
Twitter: @WorldEdBooks
YouTube: World Editions

PART ONE

In which a young woman talks on the phone a lot, seeks refuge in her father's parsonage, and discovers that she is a near relation of the seahorse.

MY MOTHER SAYS I should come up to her cottage now that I'm on vacation. It's hard to get to Amtoft no matter where in the country you happen to be. You have to take a train and multiple buses, each of which runs only once or twice a day. I hate buses, I say. Hate is a strong word, my mother says. I say it was crazy to invest in a cottage in Amtoft if she ever expected to see her family on vacations and holidays. She talks about the Limfjord and the peaceful nature up there. I say that the crabs in the Limfjord are actually known to be the most aggressive in Denmark. My mother calls me her darling and says I'm too negative. I say that I'm just relaying information about bad bus connections and Danish reptiles. Crustaceans, my mother's husband yells in the background. I say they have claws no matter what you want to call them, and my girlfriend's a zookeeper so I'm probably better informed about these kinds of things than you. She trains sea lions, my mother says, not crabs. I light a cigarette. My mother says that there's something called google maps on the internet, and that I should really try to get some transportation advice. I say that I'm well aware of google maps. She starts to spell it out. I know how to spell google, I say. Maps dot google dot com, her husband yells. D-O-T, my mother says. I breathe in. My mother is afraid that I'll never be able to find Amtoft. She talks about my sense of direction and how it's unbelievable that someone could be so frequently disoriented. I ask her if she thinks I'm good at anything at all. She says that I could speak with excellent pronunciation when I was only a year and a half old. On the other hand, you couldn't walk until you were almost three, my mother says, which was sort of awkward at mommy group, but we love our children regardless of their abilities. Your nurse had never seen a child with such poor motor skills, she says, at one point she suspected developmental issues. I don't say anything. It's nothing to be ashamed of, she says, and you don't have any trouble walking today, think about all the people out there with muscular dystrophy. At least they get money from charity organizations, I say. My mother tells me she's reading a fantastic thriller. Sounds thrilling, I say. My mother says that I'm a snob, a total snob, and that if I absolutely insist on being so elitist then I also have to stop listening to Shu-bi-dua. You've got to be consistent. I say that in that case I should probably steer clear of Amtoft as well. Now now, darling, she says with a laugh. She's been thinking that it would be fun for us to start planning her sixtieth birthday party. She talks about invitations and flowers arrangements and seating charts. It's almost a year away, I say. Ten and a half months, my mother says. That's longer than it takes from conception to birth, I say, I think we'll manage. You're just like your father, my mother says, always so last-minute. She wants me to call her when I get to Aalborg so she can help me find the right train. I say that I traveled around India for a year by myself, so maybe I'll be able to handle it. She says you can't compare India and Amtoft like that. I say that she might be right. Mothers usually are, my mother says.

*

Before I slam the door behind me I scream that she's about to make the mistake of a lifetime. Possibly, she said, but there's nothing else we can do. There's always something else we can do. Well I don't want to do anything else, she says, I'm not happy. You can't be happy all the time, misery is a condition of human existence, I yell, haven't you read Camus. She talks about how we're at two different places in our lives. I say that we're in exactly the same place, that I'm standing right in front of her in our living room, and that she should stop using spatial metaphors. Remember to breathe, she says, handing me my asthma spray. I ask her if it's about children. Partly, she says. Okay, fine, then let's have a baby. I throw out my arms and accidentally knock over a houseplant. The pot gets a crack. Adds character, I say, very important these days, things don't need to be so polished anymore, the rustic look is in. She says, while she sweeps soil up from the floor, that I'm not ready to have children. Actually I feel incredibly ready, I can literally hear the ticking of my biological clock, I say. She says it's not just that, it's also about our age difference. Good lord, I say, ten years, imagine all the couples throughout history with an age gap way bigger than ours, off the top of my head there's Simon and Janni Spies, there's Joseph and the Virgin Mary, and the list goes on, I say, because I can't think of any more. This is about us, she says. Ulrik Wilbek wrote a book called Our Differences Make Us Stronger, I say, you should read it. Ulrik Wilbek is a handball coach, she says, this is about a relationship. Teamwork is teamwork, I say. Oh be quiet, she says. I ask her when she started drawing boundaries in her life. She doesn't say anything.

*

I'm sitting in my father's living room. I look over at the church where he works. He looks tired when he gets home. I wish midnight mass could be held at some other time, he says. I have a Pink Floyd record on. Hey you, would you help me carry the stone, open your heart, I'm coming home, I sing, making my hands into a funnel in front of my mouth. My father pats me on the head and turns the music up a little. I say that she can't leave me like this, that I'm not the kind of person who gets broken up with. My father hums a little and sits down on the chair across from me. He looks around the room, at my trash bags full of clothes and the Karen Blixen poster I hung up where his Asger Jorn print used to be. My father opens a bottle of wine and puts two glasses on the table. I say she's so goddamn ignorant about literature and women and pretty much everything else. He looks panicked, like someone thinking: uh oh, here come the tears, and he reaches for a deck of cards. He clears his throat and says that I should see it as an opportunity to do something I've never had the chance to do before. Great, I say, now I have the opportunity to become a drug-addled prostitute in Berlin, and I can write a book about my misery and pain like Christiane F. He deals us seven cards each and writes our names down on a piece of paper. All right, he says, let's play 500. I say I could also just go drown myself in a river. That'd show her. He says that death by drowning is supposed to be the worst way to go, as he wins after just two rounds, which isn't terribly hard given that he has three jokers. I glare at his cards, seething. He pours more wine into my glass. My father says that everything comes to an end. I drink the wine in three swallows and mutter awful things about women while I deal the next hand. My father doesn't disagree with my assessment. This time he wins after three rounds and I'm left with minus one hundred and thirty-five points. My father looks a little alarmed. He talks about strategy and probability and how it's important not to just wait for a specific card. I look out the window. He shuffles the cards and says it's not his place to tell me what to do. About the relationship, that is. He talks about priorities and compromises and about not taking one another for granted. I remind him that he's been married three times. So was the priestly poet Thomas Kingo, my father says. Transported by his own words, he carries on about spontaneous walks in the forest, casual displays of affection, and openness, that's the most important thing, my father says, openness. I nod as he wins for the third time in a row. My father looks apologetic, which only compounds the humiliation of losing. He lights my cigarette and pours more wine into my glass. Do you have any wafers to go with this, I say. I look over at my moving boxes stacked up in the living room. He talks about what it's like to be young, about how members of the church's youth group also seem unmoored to him. He seems to be possessed by the ghost of Tine Bryld, which makes me nervous. I drop my head into my hands. He pats my hair and I feel like a dog. Like that one from the marmalade ads with the melancholy eyes. I look up at him and ask what kind of dog I would be if I were a dog. He looks confused. You're not a dog, he says. I say you never know. He says that's true and that I would probably be a labrador. I can tell from his expression that he wants me to ask why. Why, I ask. Because it's my favorite dog, he says, smiling. I assume he means it as a compliment of sorts; the labrador trots out of the room, along with Tine Bryld, and it's just the two of us again. I say that everything I touch falls apart. He looks at the wine glass in my hand with a shocked expression. I look at him. He's such a good father. I wonder if the government pays him to put up with me, if there's some kind of disability benefit for particularly beleaguered parents. He says that's not how it works, that you love your children no matter what. He hums a little melody and looks at me expectantly. I recognize some of the notes from The Old Gardener's Song. The lyrics say something about letting light and happiness in.

*

My mother has just gotten home from the cottage. She wants to show me a slideshow from Amtoft. I know what your cottage looks like, I say. Here's me sitting in the garden, my mother says, pointing at a picture. Is that so, I say. Here we are grilling on the beach, my mother says. She shows me a picture of her husband flipping a steak with a smile on his face. I see, I say. Something's wrong, my mother says, I can hear it in your voice. I shake my head and look away. You can't hide anything from your mother, my mother says. Her eyes are beaming and she looks like a detective searching for clues in a murder case. I guess I'm just not suited to be in a relationship, I say slowly. My mother says that this is common in only children, that I may have gotten too much attention as a child. I see, I say. She strokes my cheek. I've moved to the parsonage, I say. Are you very sad, she asks. I nod. Now my mother looks sad too. Have you talked about it with your doctor, she asks. I doubt he'd be able to convince her that we're meant to be together, I say. My mother asks me if I've become fatalistic, and she says that there's no such thing as the one and only. It's a social construct, she says, and she starts talking about the film industry and the flower industry and how else can they make a living. My mother starts calculating exactly how many Danish citizens there are with whom I could potentially become romantically involved. She divides the number of partners I've had by the number of years since I became sexually active. That's roughly 1.5 per year, she says, if you include that Arabic guy. There are plenty of people left, my mother says. She mentions people from my network, names of friends she's heard me talk about, and she throws in a few celebrities she thinks might be worth considering. She says she's always found Prince William so captivating. He just got married, I say. Kate's a flash in the pan, my mother says, and so dull that she blends in with the wallpaper. I say that I refuse to discuss why I'm not married to Prince William. It's all about mindset, my mother says, you've got to be open. It sounds like you're trying to sell me an apartment, I say, you've been corrupted by your occupation, why does everything you say have to sound like a slogan. It's life experience talking, my mother says. She asks what my plans are now. I'm going to let myself go to the dogs, I say, or to a cloister, maybe in the Himalayas. You can't do that, she says, you've got no sense of direction, if you think it's hard to get to Amtoft then you'll never find your way to the Himalayas. Your father and I will have to go searching for you with Interpol and we'll probably end up on some television show about missing children. She raises her eyebrows. And you know how slow your father is, we'll be late for the flight and we'll drive each other crazy before we even get to the airport. She sighs and says she can see that it's a mess. I'll have to redo the whole seating chart for my birthday party, your girlfriend was the only person who could stand talking to Aunt Jette. I ruin everything, I say. You know what darling, my mother says, I'll just put Aunt Jette at the end of the table, *kein Problem*. My mother closes the slideshow. I hate it when people disappear from my life, I say. Hate is a strong word, my mother says. She opens a window and turns on the kitchen hood. You can smoke inside today, my mother says.

*

The yellow walls of my doctor's waiting room are hung with an array of landscape prints. A crystal vase of sunflowers sits on the table. Beside me are a rocking horse and two plastic boxes full of blocks. I build a little tower on the table, and when there are no blocks left I make a roof out of a little pamphlet on seasonal allergies. I accidentally bump the lowest block and the tower topples, knocking the vase over on its way down. My tower lies on the table like an abandoned ruin flooded by the water pouring out of the vase. I gather up the sunflowers into a little bouquet. I hold the flowers and stare at the broken glass. A man comes over from reception and looks at me. He says my name questioningly and offers me his hand. I shake it with the hand without sunflowers in it. He introduces himself and tells me to come with him. I follow him into an office. My doctor sits down in a chair across from me and asks how he can help me. I realize that I still have the sunflowers in my hand and I put them down on his table. He gets a white coffee mug and fills it with water. While he arranges the flowers I try to imagine how he could possibly help me. I remember one time when I sat next to a doctor at a wedding. My dining partner was an ear, nose, and throat doctor. As a courtesy I asked him his favorite diagnosis. After a lengthy monologue he finally concluded that it was probably Kartagener's syndrome, which has something to do with abnormal cilia. One type of cilia is the microscopic hairs coating your airways, he whispered as if he were sharing confidential information. I stubbed out my cigarette. The condition is often seen in children suffering from recurring sinusitis, he explained. I imagined a sinusitis to be a lesser-known dinosaur roaming the tundra. I informed my dining partner that the baroque was an extremely interesting period in literary history because it was in many ways a precursor to postmodernism. He smiled benevolently and said that it would be interesting to do a study where you x-rayed children's thoraxes. I said that the thorax was a species of dinosaur and asked him if he'd seen Jurassic Park. He laughed smugly and said that the thorax is actually the rib cage, and that patients with Kartagener's syndrome have situs inversus, which is a condition where the patient's vital organs are situated in reverse, like a reflection. I said that reflections are interesting indeed, that the poets of the baroque used reflections as a way to express the multidimensionality of the world. He said situs inversus seems to be the result of abnormalities in the cilia, which have been detected as early as the embryonic phase known as gastrulation. I nodded and said the poets of the baroque employed many symbols of vanitas, so he wouldn't think he was the only one who could say something in Latin. The soap bubble was a common leitmotif, I said, signifying the fleeting nature of time. He looked at me, clearly annoyed, but he regained his composure and explained that these abnormal cilia are unable to maintain the flow of embryonic fluid. I said that like the thinkers of the baroque, postmodernism insists upon conveying the fragility of life, albeit with a very different mode of expression. Which, he said, is exactly what leads to situs inversus.

*

My doctor clears his throat and asks why I'm here. I rarely lie just to avoid uncomfortable situations, I see it more as a narrative obligation. I talk vaguely about stomach pains, mysterious muscle spasms in my abdomen. It really hurts, I say. When I look up I get caught in his penetrating green gaze. He looks at me gravely, nodding rhythmically. The silence lasts a little too long and I'm seized by a sudden urge to tell him every secret I've ever had. I say that I cheated on my girlfriend once but I was really drunk and I've regretted it ever since, that I've never read Crime and Punishment but I always pretend I have. All things considered, I say, I'm not doing very well these days. He raises his eyebrows, gives me a brief smile, and nods in silence. I say that my girlfriend left me and that I have a really hard time letting people go. I have an unnaturally strong memory which prevents me from moving on with my life, I say. My doctor says that the conscious transfer of memories from short term to long term happens in a region of the brain known as the hippocampus, meaning seahorse in Latin, which is the shape that part of the brain resembles. Remembering is a creative process that builds on the ability to recreate situations, he says, what seems like a factual event is actually a construction of the mind. Are you saying I'm lying, I ask. Distortions and unconscious omissions are a natural part of the process of memory. I tell him that when Mozart was only fourteen he transcribed an entire choral piece from memory after hearing it performed in the Sistine Chapel. I ask if some people have bigger seahorses than others. Maybe my seahorse is gigantic, I say. My doctor says that memories are stored by one of two different brain functions, depending on whether they have emotional content or not. The hippocampus is used for consciously emotional memories, while the amygdala, which is almond-shaped, lies in the core of the brain and holds implicit memories. I say that I must have more than one seahorse swimming around in there. Perhaps Mozart's almond wasn't oversized, he says, perhaps the eyewitnesses and the later corroborators of the event were so impressed by the boy's musicality that they forgot how he mixed up a few of the baritone lines or fudged a harmony or altered a cadence ever so slightly. I say it's worrisome that human history depends on a horde of seahorses stampeding through time. When you get down to it, my doctor says, that's how it is. Seahorses have no stomachs, so they constantly have to suck up everything around them until they drop dead, I say. And female seahorses are the worst, the only group among all the ray-finned fishes to foist the task of childbearing onto the males. They can't even be bothered to reproduce. Nothing ever really leaves their bodies, I say, and that's exactly what it's like to be me. He says that hippocampus is just a name. So there's a seahorse in my brain who rules over all my memories, I say. My doctor nods and says one could put it that way.

*

I pound on her door late one night. She looks very tired, and she steps aside and points to the sofa. I say that I moved in with my father. What about your parents, I ask, are they happy now. She says she hasn't talked to them. Then you really ought to call them, I say, handing her my phone. You should never pass up an opportunity to make your parents happy, it says so in the Bible: fourth commandment, Book of Exodus. She sighs and hands me a cup of coffee. I can just picture it, I say, how they'll dance through their fields whooping to the sky in a fit of joyful delirium. Maybe they'll even throw a party, I say, and make a big doll that looks like me and burn it over a bonfire. I doubt that, she says. Oh come on, I say, your mother's so creative. I accidentally knock the cup over and coffee spills out onto my dress. I scream, and the cup hits the floor and breaks into pieces. She takes my skirt off and puts a towel soaked in cold water over my thighs. Do you seriously think they'd throw a party because we broke up. I haven't broken anything, I say, you're the one abandoning me. I study the red splotches on my thighs. She starts picking up the shards from the floor. Last year they put on that strange festival where your dad ran around with a sword and made weird noises while your mom wore plastic horns on her head and taught people folk dances, I say. It was a Viking convention, she says. One thing I don't understand is why your family eats fish on every holiday, I say. You're not even from West Jutland. Did you ever stop to consider that the fish is symbol of Christ, I say, that you're sitting there gorging yourselves on Jesus. And when your mom grills fish their eyes always melt, I say, they drip down onto the charcoal almost rhythmically. You have no idea how many times I almost threw up at those get-togethers. She says that's what happens when a fluid substance is exposed to heat. Can you imagine cleaning that grill, I say, standing there at the sink and washing fish eyes down the drain. You're a zookeeper for god's sake, I say. Then I talk for a while about the World Wildlife Fund. My skin burns. She gets a bag of ice cubes, packs them into a dishrag and puts it on my thighs. She says that the codfish has muscles within its ears and if you cut through them you can see exactly how long it's been alive. Just like the rings on a tree. Fascinating, I say. She takes the ice cubes away and touches the red splotches, and I notice that she's put my dress in warm water. She pours some white powder onto her palm. Have you started doing heroin now, I say, have you been seeing that drug addict who was always trying to sleep with you. Vanish Oxi Action, she says with a sigh. Stains rejected, colors protected, I say. It's white, she says, so there's not much to protect. I don't know what to do with myself, I say, everything I touch falls apart, I feel like an elephant in a glass shop. There's nothing wrong with elephants, she says, they're highly intelligent and they have the best memories in all the animal kingdom. Inside the elephant there's a seahorse who rules over every memory, I say. She puts a blanket over me and holds my hand until I fall asleep on the sofa.

Monologues of a Seahorse I

Within my heart there is a building, a dusty museum of broken hearts and lovers past. There are long, winding hallways and countless collections in which you are displayed according to year. You are living marble statues, snow-white, casting long shadows, and I examine you in detail on my all-too-frequent restless wanderings, like a worn-out tour guide who, with a grudging sense of devotion, endeavors to maintain a degree of order. I tidy a French braid, pick up a piece of sheet music from the floor, brush a speck of dust off of a shoulder. You are all frozen stiff in the poses I remember best. You with your neck leaning back and your eyes closed, blowing into your saxophone, and you with snow in your hair, bursting into laughter, and you with your melancholy eyes and your hand reaching out to me. And you, still crying, your hair falling across your face, and you, suspended in the middle of a dance step. And you with a dart in your hand and a look of dark concentration, and you with all your theories about the world, trapped in a still-trembling gesture. And you, silently swallowed by your own thoughts, standing up straight with an absent gaze, one foot propped on your opposite knee, as if you were resting on yourself. And you with the Big Dipper drawn across your cheek in moles, your smile so serious in the darkness, and you, sitting up in your combine harvester behind a fountain of flying grain. I try to systematize you, make chronological sequences. I think of you as a line of royal succession. I have a collection for summer loves, spun out of sunshine and restlessness, and another for winter romances, conjured by snowflakes and schnapps. Other rooms are dedicated to the people who took me by surprise, to those who surprise me still, and to people who showed up at the wrong time, whose performances were obscured by others from the same season or period. They drift between the rooms, evading my categories. In the adjacent halls there are people who would wonder why they came to be here, exhibited in my museum. An aloof professor from Aarhus University who spent twenty years of his life researching dependent clauses, various people I've seen at bus stops or met in stairways. The unwitting recipients of unrequited love built on silent musings and spurious notions of fleeting reciprocity. You take each other's places, enhance one another, and the strength of my feelings is directly proportional to the extent of my boredom. There is a VIP collection, a secluded room for the few people I can't even distinguish from myself. You give each other furtive nods; you know exactly why you're here. I want to apologize to you all, to confess my bizarre behavior once and for all through a megaphone while awaiting your forgiveness. Or I could issue detailed apologies in hushed tones to each and every one of you, for putting you on display, for freezing you fast in these never-ending movements.

I WAIT FOR my best friend Mulle in The Old Town. We meet in the Renaissance Garden. Mulle's long red hair flies behind her like a dragon's tail. The freckles around her nose fill me with an urge to connect the dots to find out what picture would emerge across her face. She runs over to me and embraces me tightly. Her hair falls over my eyes, and I look out at the world through an orange veil. What did the priest have to say, she asks. I say that he didn't say much, but that we're in the middle of the world's longest game of 500. He's beating me by seven thousand points, I say, why does he always win. Mulle takes my hand and pulls me toward an ice-cream stand. I'm the one in need of an uplifting victory, I say, my heart's been dashed to atoms. Mulle doesn't like talking about feelings, but she does buy me a cotton candy. What about your mom, Mulle asks. She started carrying on about Prince William again, I say. He's been a person of interest for a while now, Mulle says. Three and a half years, Mulle, I say, and I stick three fingers into the air and with the other hand I make a half-circle with my thumb and my index finger. Okay, Mulle says, taking my hands, so where do we stand. My favorite thing about Mulle is her strong team spirit. We're standing in The Old

Town, I say, my mouth full of pink fluff. I tell her she should stop using spatial metaphors. Do we hate her, or do we want her back, Mulle asks. We don't hate anyone, I say, it's not allowed in my family. So we want her back, Mulle says. I nod. Mulle is my spin doctor. Then we need to strategize, she says. Mulle studies political science and she likes to put things into systems and diagrams. The whole world can fit onto a coordinate plane, Mulle says, so what are her demands. Children and all that stuff, I say. We're not prepared for that, Mulle says. She's not getting any children, we're firm on that, but maybe you can make some other concessions when we get to the bargaining table, Mulle says. She also wants a pet, I say, and you know how I hate animals. A goldfish, Mulle says, maybe a turtle, animals that don't say anything. She wants a furry animal, I say. If your woman wants an animal then we'll have to get her an animal, Mulle says, she needs to feel that we're making an effort to fix the relationship. She also seems to think I'm way too intense, I say. Then we'll make a more palatable edition of you, Mulle says, we'll start smoking out the window, we'll tone your obnoxious behaviors down a notch. I think she regards me as a fine exemplar of my genre, I say, it's just that she's looking for something else entirely. That's trickier, says Mulle, in fact it undermines our entire negotiation strategy. I nod. This process has probably been underway for a while, Mulle says. I think about it for a minute and then I say I probably should've seen it coming. I just hoped I'd wake up one morning and suddenly want all the same things she wanted, I say, picking some cotton candy out of my hair. We're not even close to being thirty, Mulle says, having kids is something you do when you've given up on achieving anything else in this world, it's the ultimate spasmodic attempt to find meaning in your life. Her mind is made up, I say, she almost never makes up her mind, but when she finally does there's no changing it. Then maybe this is for the best, my spin doctor says, and she puts her arm around me. My tears drip down into the cotton candy. It looks like rain falling on a landscape of pink snow.

*

I say that I want to keep the organ pipes her grandfather made. On our refrigerator there's a black-and-white photograph of an old man. He's smiling. He has a checkered cap on his head and a piece of wood in his hands. He's been smiling at me for years from his perch on the refrigerator door. You never even met my grandfather, she says. Sometimes it's actually more painful to miss someone you never knew, I say, there's a strange feeling of emptiness when your nostalgia has nothing to grasp on to. That was something I'd heard at some point on a TV show about adoption. She sighs. I run my hands over the organ pipes. You always said you thought they were ugly, she says. Well they're not exactly beautiful, I say, but I've grown attached to them so it would be unacceptable if I didn't get at least one pipe. This is what happens when you break up, I say, you divide your assets. I say that she owes me something, that she robbed me of three and a half years of my youth.

Imagine all the people I could've slept with if it weren't for you, I say. Thirty a year, I say, maybe fifty if I started wearing makeup. The least you could do is give me an organ pipe. But you don't like casual sex, she says wearily. Don't start acting like you know me, I say, maybe you don't know me at all. Maybe I'm secretly a psychopath and I've been living a double life you know nothing about. She looks out the window and says she doesn't think that's the case. From the window you can see a sliver of sea. I ask why she always has to be so undramatic. I guess it's just my nature, she says. It's one of the things I like best about her, but I don't say that. I blow a little into the organ pipes and a strange sound comes out. I say I'm sure her grandfather would've wanted me to have them. She says that in any event her grandfather would've liked me. She looks out into the distance and I can't tell whether she's thinking about me or her grandfather. I say that's a weird thing to say in the middle of a fight. Are we fighting, she asks. I take the organ pipes down from the wall and say that I'm taking them home with me. Oh wait, I say, I don't have a home. She rubs my arm.

Monologues of a Seahorse II

Inside my ear there is a snail shell playing an interminable symphony. An assemblage of melodies set on repeat and broadcast through my neural pathways at high volumes. You are the voices in my head, various dialects and languages braided together, speaking to me. Accents from Aarhus, Northern Jutland, Fyn, and Copenhagen. Hindi, Norwegian, Italian, and Arabic. A hoarse voice, the sound of a saxophone that is not hers, or the tones of a classical concert in a bright room where you should have been. The sound of the sea and your bare feet dancing in the waves where Kattegat meets Skagerrak. Your fingers hitting the keyboard, the faint sound of brushstrokes across a canvas, your stilettos on the cobblestones, resounding like a shotgun. And you with your soundlessness, you are a chain of exclamation points, that is how I think of you, like eyes and hands and exclamation points and soundlessness. And all your favorite words and expressions, your metaphors and recurring themes, your pauses and delays, your rhetoric and your truths, your breathing and your silence. The noises people make when dragging a chair across the floor, when coming through a doorway, when closing a cabinet. When your silence is broken by long monologues and the words are bound together by your hands which fly around the room. And you with your unbridled laughter. The loud, rhythmic sounds that turn into a picture and spread throughout your body. The neck you lean back, the lips you part, your eyes that vanish into little crevices. I need this laughter so much. I tell you the most ludicrous stories, lying and exaggerating to bring forth your sounds. I tickle you, nibble your ear, show you silly clips from old films, read long passages from books, all to keep you laughing for eternity. Your fingers drumming impatiently against the table, the bells tied to the hundreds of braids in your hair, the sound of your voice calling out in a foreign language as you sleep. Shot glasses of whiskey clinking against each other, the crack in your voice the moment before you lose control. Your long pointless stories, these sudden parades of associations, these colorful lies, begotten as quickly as you can say them. You talk and talk as the stories unfurl, your voice rising and falling, your blinking eyes and flashing pupils reflecting every shift of feeling. The sound of the way you repress your laughter, the fact that you can laugh without a sound. Your voices when they call to me, say my name, scream my name, whisper my name.

I TELL MY doctor that I've been hearing voices. He looks worried and talks about various destructive coping mechanisms. I attempt to decipher the movements of his lips, and try to guess the next word before he says it. It's a little quiz I give myself. I'm captivated by my doctor's voice, it's all I can think about today, even when he's not saying anything. I'm always on the verge of confessing it, and I have to think of other things, of fruits, of toys, of childhood memories. He speaks slowly, as if considering every word, and his cadences are songlike. He sings of cognitive structures. I wonder whether he listens to the content of his words or if it's a chant he's memorized, and if that explains the rhythm of his sentences. My doctor asks what the voices tell me. I say that they don't speak in complete sentences, it's more like I'm haunted by sounds of the past. My doctor looks relieved and talks about tinnitus. He tells me about a defect in the tiny sensory receptors within the cochlea that causes our neurons to start sending erroneous signals to the auditory nerve. He sings a little song about noise damage and hereditary hearing loss. My doctor looks at me and asks what I'm thinking. The more I want to talk to someone, the harder it is. My phrasing becomes clumsy and I feel like I'm drooling. I adhere to an internal logic void of discernable coherence, and nothing sounds the way I want it to. My father has a book about Victor Borge called A Smile Is the Shortest Distance. I'm skeptical of the smile; it's the Western world's most overrated muscle contraction after the orgasm. For me, the shortest distance between two people is an imprudent sentence which ought to have remained unspoken. I'm thinking about how entrancing your voice is, I say.

*

I'm reading on a bench in Vennelystparken when my phone rings. Hi darling, it's mom, she screeches. I put my book down. She's in Amtoft and she thinks I should come for a visit during my fall break. I never get to see you, she sighs. I say that she's exaggerating. She says that exaggeration runs in our family along the maternal line. Exaggeration isn't a genetically determined trait, her husband mumbles in the background. She tells him it's impossible to know for sure, since today's young people are so thoroughly indifferent to their genetic origins. I say that I'm a healthy, fully functional person, and, following a satisfactory childhood and a completed education, I've now established my own life. People always need their mothers, my mother says. Naturally, I say, but only to a limited extent in my case, and you ought to be pleased about that. I look down at the lake, where a young man in a wheelchair is feeding the ducks. Imagine if I were developmentally challenged or autistic or paralyzed from the neck down, I say. My mother says that paralyzed people can lead very fulfilling lives, and that the autistic are sweet. I ask if she has a problem with the fact that I'm not autistic. She says the only problem she has with me is that I never come to visit. Never say never, I say. My mother sighs. I say she should consider herself lucky that I'm an ordinary, functioning individual with healthy interests and a natural ability to enter into committed relationships. It doesn't seem to be going so well with those committed relationships, my mother says. I say that my parents' divorce and the many disappointments of my childhood have likely made it difficult for me to form bonds with other people. My mother disagrees, and she says that I'll miss her when she's just a faded portrait on the wall. Without a doubt, I say. The man in the wheelchair rolls away from the lake in silence, with four ducks following him in a little procession. I tell my mother that if she gives me a small portrait of herself then I'll find a nice sunny place for it, to achieve the most elegant fade possible.

*

I lie on my father's sofa watching Days of Our Lives. Tony isn't Tony after all, but rather his identical cousin who's been posing as Tony for twenty years. The cousin has been holding Tony captive for all that time. You can't count on anything in this world of ours, I say to my father, taking a handful of cheese puffs. The crunching echoes inside my head so that I can't hear. I turn up the volume on the TV. My father's wife plays the piano a little louder. You can always count on your father, my father says. I smile at him. I try to eat some cheese puffs while also smoking a cigarette. Both the smoke and the cheese puffs go down the wrong way. It's important to move on, my father says, slapping my back, you've got to get back in the saddle. I say I'll get back in it tomorrow, but my father and his wife insist on taking me with them to a concert. Pink Floyd Project, my father says, they're almost as good as the original. I say that's not quite how I'd imagined moving on. My father asks what I'm going to do instead. I say that I'm going to reduce her to a memory, brutally and pitilessly. I'm going to feel a discreet and measured affection for her, and I'll allow myself moments of sentimentality around New Year's and quick glimpses of her face when I've been drinking. Which you often are, my father says, lighting his pipe. When she does appear in my recollections, I say, she'll stand on an even footing with any other occurrence in my life, and I'll tell everyone around me that what doesn't kill us makes us stronger, and they'll all concur and think I'm handling the situation with the utmost grace. Is that so, my father's wife says. I'll tell them that happiness lies in our own hands, and that we've got to enjoy our youth, and I'll say it in the same incontrovertible way that you say bless you when someone sneezes, like an automatic gesture, nothing more than a courtesy, I say. That sounds like a good plan, my father says, but in the meantime let's go to a concert. My father's wife turns off the TV, gives me a pat on the cheek, and says it'll be good for me to get out of the house.

*

I sit a little ways away from my father and his wife and watch them swaying simultaneously to the music. A young man comes up and asks if I'd like a beer. My father straightens his back and comes over and shakes his hand. The young man asks if it's all right if he sits down beside me. My father's wife says yes. The young man says I have pretty eyes. My father nods. I say that his comment is untrustworthy, considering how dark it is. My father smiles at the young man and drums on his glass with three fingers. My father's wife nudges me and says that the young man looks sweet. Somehow I like that she doesn't bother whispering. He's a man, I say. He's a person, my father's wife says, aren't you a humanist? Humanists hate people, I say, they only like the idea of them. The young man smiles in confusion. I hope he's very drunk. He pulls me aside a little and says that my parents seem young at heart. Incredibly young, I say. He asks me if I'd like to drink a cup of coffee with him sometime next week. The young man says that he doesn't have any suspicious intentions. I say it's suspicious to say that you don't have any suspicious intentions. Like how you can't say articulate without articulating, I say. My father clears his throat and says that I've always been very interested in language. My father's wife says there's no harm in going out for a cup of coffee. I say that once I heard about someone who choked to death when his coffee went down the wrong way. My father says that doesn't happen very often. All the same, I say, it's a risk.

*

The young man calls me a few days later and says it was nice to meet me. He says that he had a good time, and that he'd like to get to know me better. Actually, I don't think you would, I say slowly. I hear alarm bells going off. I'm not saying I never get the urge to braid my hair and don a flowery apron. I imagine how, if he got sick, I'd take care of him just like Florence Nightingale. I'd make tea and buy him flowers and menthol cigarettes even though he doesn't smoke, and I'd tell him that nicotine numbs the cilia within the throat and relieves every cough. In the summer we'd grill together in the garden, and he'd say I love you periodically and in appropriate settings, and I'd say can you believe this rain or ask him if he knew the time. In moments of especial sentimentality I'd long to bear him a bevy of children. Then I'd crush their sandcastles when we went to the beach and, with a hoarse cackle, I'd yell that Santa Claus doesn't exist, robbing them of their childish beliefs. And my children would make strange things for me in arts and crafts, which they would wrap up and give me for Christmas with beaming eyes, and I'd say what do we need more coasters for, they're simply too bourgeois, a few stains won't hurt the table, they add character you know. I'd forget to pack their lunches, and he would hire an au pair from Eastern Europe, most likely named Milagros, who the children would start calling mom after a few weeks. And at parent-teacher conferences I'd be painfully bored and I'd complain about not being able to smoke on school grounds, and he'd bake casseroles and become an active member of the PTA and hold my hand while I stared indecorously at the other mothers' breasts. I'd flirt shamelessly with the parents of my children's playmates and I'd say let's have a little glass of wine while they play, and by the time he got home we'd be making out on the sofa. One Sunday morning I'd abandon them all. He'd be crushed, but Milagros would see it as her big chance to get a residence permit, and they'd be married within a year. I'd take him to court, claim he was psychologically unstable, and insinuate that Milagros was a heroin addict (you know those Eastern European girls), and I'd get full custody in a heartbeat. Then I'd drink myself to death while the children languished in a reformatory. He says my name through the phone. I hang up.

Monologues of a Seahorse III

Inside my diaphragm there is a nightclub. You dance around on my bottom rib, and you lean up against my spine while you talk with drinks in both your hands. Maybe you're telling old stories and saying, I know, she's such an only child, and she always got mad when I said so, really, she never gave me anything besides books for my birthday either, oh yes, Tove Ditlevsen's collected works, I got that one too. Would you come to blows, those of you who were contemporaries, or would you dance the tango and lean into one another with mutual compassion, because you'd all had to endure me? Like people who witness the same traffic accident or fight in the same war and become friends for life. Or would you talk about me with the cloying affection of people speaking of the dead. Would there be occasional songs and little skits? Would you drink gin and tonics for sentimental reasons, and dance to Danish hits from the eighties, we are caught fast in your inner universe, you'd sing. Regardless, I know you'd end up listening to Bob Dylan or Leonard Cohen or Miles Davis or whoever it was you were always raving about, because you take music very seriously, and you always look very serious when you say that you take music very seriously, and it's so easy just to come up with a catchy melody. You'd talk about the musicality, the timelessness, the poetry, and, laughing a raspy, elitist laugh, you'd commiserate together about how frustrating it was that I didn't get it. I wonder whether you're all quite similar, both those of you who held on to me for an instant and those by whom I was captivated at length. It would make for a strange party, because most of you talk considerably less than I do. You'd all mill about, waiting for someone else to start a conversation, and you'd miss me at the beginning, like irrelevant background noise or muzak in a supermarket. The worst, of course, would be when you started comparing your stacks of love letters only to discover that they all say more or less the same thing and not always in a different way, that I actually engaged in the copy-pasting of specific passages. I wonder how many of you there would be at this party, I'm afraid the guest list may reach into the hundreds. Some of you still make me happy, others melancholy, and a few still send me into a rage, as you promenade around to the rhythms of my diaphragm. Garlands of nerve threads hang from my sternum, above which rise the walls of my heart. Your shyness quickly dissipates as the gin bottles run dry, and you sing karaoke with your arms around one another. Respect, you sing, and I Will Survive, and you feel strong and indestructible, because within the walls of my heart there is a disco ball, and you fling yourselves around in the glittering light as you dance the boogie-woogie, like a conglomeration of blurry colors, and in the end I can't even tell any of you apart.

I LIE IN my mother's garden. Leaves fly around in the air and briefly land on the brick sidewalk, like a brown-stained red carpet. My mother bustles around and moves big mountains of colors across the lawn, humming all the while. I'd like you to write a birthday card to your aunt Jette, she says. I get up and take out a cigarette. My mother waves the smoke away with frantic movements, though I haven't lit it yet. She talks about how incredibly happy it would make my aunt Jette to get a birthday card from me. My mother says that she knows this from personal experience, and that her own birthday is right around the corner. It's eight months away, I say, you sound like a little child. My mother reminds me of all the birthday cards my aunt has sent me over the years. I say that I can't be compelled by the birthday cards that others have chosen to send. All the same, my mother says. I say that I remember my aunt Jette's birthday cards, they were always filled with endless descriptions of the birds on her porch. My mother says that people who don't have children have to cultivate other interests. You can do that if you do have children too, I say. My mother talks about my aunt, who she also thinks is a bit on the odd side. I say that there was always something a tad deranged about her bird fixation, and that I hate birthday cards about birds, and also birds in general. My mother says that hate is a strong word. She talks on and on about lonely childless women, and I say that I'll write a birthday card to my aunt. It'll have a big picture of a bird on the front, and on the envelope I'll draw birds instead of cakes and presents, and inside it there will be a dead bird, like the Italian mafia, I say. That was fish, her husband yells through the kitchen window, they sent dead fish. I've never cared for fish either, my mother says. It's a symbol of Christ, I say. My mother says that I sound like my father. Why do you always have to be so strange, darling, my mother asks. At least I'm not a vegetarian, I say. No, your diet is so unhealthy, my mother says, you have a concerning relationship with food. I say that food is a strong word. My mother sighs and says that you always love your children, no matter who they turn out to be. I say that that kind of remark is reserved for the mothers of criminals and drug addicts. She says that smoking is a form of drug addiction.

*

Mulle and I are drinking beers at a pub in The Old Town. My mother says I'm just whining, but I'm not, I say. Maybe a little, Mulle says, you have a particular talent for broadcasting your suffering to the world. Nonsense, I say. It was the same when we were kids, Mulle says, you'd make a huge scene whenever you had to rip off a band-aid. Mulle starts pulling an imaginary band-aid up off her knee. Ever so carefully, you'd pinch the outer edge with your fingertips and the minutes would become longer than they were, you drew out every moment as the band-aid heaved your skin up in little mounds, she says. Ow, ow, the world is so cruel, Mulle whines in a baby voice while rubbing her knee. Every single little hair on your skin would be slowly torn loose, and you'd take as many pauses as possible so as to truly relish the full duration of your pain, Mulle says, pulling and pulling in the air over her knee. Meanwhile, the priest would be tearing his hair out in desperation, Mulle says, and stuffing you with chocolate to try to cheer you up. And my mother would be trying to find someone to adopt me, I say. Mulle points at herself. I always rip band-aids off with a flick of the wrist, Mulle says, waving her fingers in the air, then it's over and done with. That's exactly why you have an easier life, I say. It was the same with the tooth fairy, Mulle says. Do you still have to refer to that kind of creature as if it were real, I say. The rest of us would tie colorful threads to our loose teeth and yank them out, Mulle says, boom. She gently tugs on one of her front teeth. We'd put them in a glass on our bedside table and wait for a tooth fairy and a new tooth, Mulle says, that's how simple life can be. I was far too intelligent for all that, I say. You were disillusioned by the age of five, Mulle says. You went around for months tonguing your loose tooth, prodding at the few threads of gum that still held it in your mouth. Ow, ow, Mulle, I think I'm dyyyiiing, Mulle moans in her baby voice. I'm not like that anymore, I say, I take life's challenges head-on. Only because you don't have any baby teeth left, Mulle says. On the other hand, I do have a broken heart, I say, pointing at my chest. No doubt about that, Mulle says.

*

I call her in the middle of the night. She's out on the town. That's interesting, I say, given that for two years you never wanted to go out at night with me. I say that I thought people over thirty went to dinner parties and talked about their gutters and mortgages and epidural blocks. Wow, you must be really desperate, I say. She's out with Joy. Joy used to be a drug addict, I say, Joy's not the one for you. We're just having a few beers, she says. Furthermore, I think it's quite misleading for a person with so many problems to go by the name of Joy, I say, imagine being called Joy while taking antidepressants, it's quite the paradox. She says that Joy's parents couldn't have known that when they named her. I hear her breathing. I can tell she's annoyed that she even entered into a debate about it. I say that in that case there's nothing stopping Joy from going to a numerologist and finding something more suitable. I suggest Lizzy. I hear a woman laughing loudly in the background. She's also boring, utterly lacking in imagination, I say, it's almost a relief to know she took drugs, at least it shows some kind of initiative, a healthy curiosity, if you will. We're just playing Yahtzee, she says, sounding tired. She asks how I'm doing. I say that it's funny she should ask, that I'm not doing so well because my girlfriend kicked me out and is presently trying to hook up with an unimaginative drug addict. Playing Yahtzee with an unimaginative drug addict, she says.

*

My doctor looks shocked when he sees my face the next morning. My nose hurts the worst, I say. My voice sounds nasal. He touches it gently and says that it's likely broken. He says that the pain is likely due to a blow to my nasal root. Or perhaps it's the pounding rhythm of all my longing, I say. He asks how it happened. I mumble something about a drug addict. He looks at me with a serious expression and asks if I've reported it. It may have been my own fault, I say. My doctor has a fatherly expression as he talks about how it's common for victims to blame themselves. He asks if it happened in connection with a robbery. In a way, I say, she was trying to sleep with my girlfriend. My doctor leans back in his chair, holding his eyes on me. I stare at his carpet. It's blue with red stripes. Didn't your girlfriend break up with you, my doctor asks. That's a question of semantics, I say, there's rarely only one single answer out there. I hold forth on social constructivism for a while. My doctor says that you can't force people to be in a romantic relationship if they themselves don't want to be. People don't always know what's best for them, I say, think about people who drink themselves to death, or smokers who gradually destroy their lungs. He raises his eyebrows. That may be the case, he says, but there does exist something called self-control. When I have no explanation for my actions I resort to literature. Noses exist, I say, nightshade exists, the dark side, the robe of namelessness exists. He asks if I've reported it to the police. I shake my head. He smiles and says that perhaps I could plead temporary insanity. Or just insanity, I say. He taps my nose lightly and says I should give it some peace and quiet.

Monologues of a Seahorse IV

Inside my solar plexus is a bookshelf lined with skulls. Skeletons always look like they're laughing, and that's how I think of you, like laughing demons beating and battering my body. You're the sum of my defeats, you're all the guilty feelings I've been stockpiling, and you march in rank and file across my pressure points, moving in tandem with my pain. You sit in my head and scream when I'm hungover, you tie ribbons around my ovaries when I have my period, and you do somersaults through my stomach when I have food poisoning. You are the yellow discharge of my eye infections and my swollen lymph nodes when I lose my voice, rejoicing over my sudden silence. It is you who've taken up residence in my wisdom teeth, and you who dance atop my bruises. It is you who admire the fountain of blood every time I cut myself with a knife. You're the nausea when I'm carsick, the suffocating feeling of my asthma attacks, and you're the big oval blister on my feet after I've bought new shoes. I hate you all, systematically and in alphabetical order, but my sorrows are all tangled together and I can't figure out whether I hate you or myself or just all of us. You with the wounded look that gave me a headache, you with that bitter twitch of the mouth when you felt badly treated, and you who never did get that divorce. You with your little glasses of vinegar which you said would absorb the smell of my cigarettes, and you with all your beautiful dreams and the way they slowly disappeared. You with your trusting eyes that made me nervous, and you who always slipped away when I had something important to say. And you who said I was noticeably prettier when I wore makeup, and you who always photographed our food when we were on vacation. Your gentle voice when you spoke about your wife, and you who always said that yelling louder doesn't make me more right. Of course it does. And you who always want to talk about feelings when I'm reading, and you who laugh at things that are objectively not funny, and you who have never been critical of anything at all. And you who say that Anne Linnet's lyrics are banal (perhaps someone is projecting) and make me feel crazy by watching pole vaulting during the Olympics, for being interested in pole vaulting at all. And you who refer to books I know you've never read. The tender notes in your voice when you talk to dogs, and the very idea that you talk to animals as if they were people. You who smile and say bless you to people you don't know, and you who never call, thereby denying me the possibility of not picking up. And you who speak more slowly when talking to people of foreign origin, rigorously articulating every word, and then accuse me of accusing you of being racist when I point it out. And you who say the most obvious things about life, thinking you're being revolutionary, things like everyone is different, or art has no boundaries. And you who say I have an immature attitude towards board games, and that you have to lose with grace, which is easy to say when you have a hotel on Rådhuspladsen. And you who drive me crazy with your Buddhistic resignation and your stubborn faith that everything happens for a reason. You are all my insecurities, you are all of the plates I've smashed in anger, you are all the newly painted benches I've sat down on and all the glasses of red wine I've spilled onto white tablecloths. You're the strangling feeling a second before I throw up, and you're the sound of the piece of music that you practiced thirty-five times a day. You're all the wearying conversations about your expectations in a relationship, and you're the high-pitched tone at the edge of your voice, rising as your rage unfurls. It's your fault that I walk through this world backwards and screaming. That I can't control the noises I make, that I stumble around, colliding head-on with people and things and natural phenomena. That I stagger in circles, that my every utterance is a scream scrawled in neon light, that even my whispers sound like thunder, and that all my emotions are unfettered and phosphorescent. That I am the mirror image of my thoughts, that I was born inside out, that I drag my guts behind me wherever I go, leaving a trail of blood through streets and houses, across furniture and beds. It is all your fault.

PART TWO

In which Christmas approaches at the old parsonage, and our heroine longs for warmer climes, while fantasizing about Kingo, stalking her doctor, and holding her course into the abyss.

WE'RE IN A store on Strøget. I need a new outfit for my cousin's wedding. I'm not doing it, I say, I won't take part in that kind of hypocrisy, I refuse to support the institution of marriage. My mother says I'm being childish, and that just because I'm having a hard time in my love life it doesn't mean my cousin doesn't deserve to get married. Marriage is a deranged ambition, I say, the idea that anyone is able to have any kind of connection at all with another person strikes me as delusional. My mother pushes me into a changing room and puts a pile of dresses onto a stool. She stands beside me and looks at us in the mirror. She says it's incredible how much I look like my father. The only difference is that he wears black dresses and you don't have a beard, my mother says, laughing. She finds this equally funny every time she says it. And what little beard you do have is hardly visible, my mother says, at least not until you get right up close. My mother says that we're probably descended from a clan of gypsies, which would explain our abundant hair growth, and that I should just be glad I didn't get her black hair and brown eyes too. People often assume she's Pakistani or Turkish, and they tell her that her Danish is very impressive and that she's open-minded for not wearing a headscarf. I try on an orange dress. It's almost real silk, my mother says, buttoning up the back of the dress. More like chiffon on a bad day, I mumble. Today is a good day, my mother says. She spins me around, inspecting me clinically. I take a purple dress down from its hanger, it's short and there are studs on the belt that goes with it. My mother says she also had terrible taste in clothes when she was my age. She says it contemplatively, as if addressing herself, though she's looking at me. My mother says that it's completely natural, and that style is something that comes with time. She walks around me in circles. My mother says I should try to accentuate my femininity. Just because you don't have hips doesn't mean you can't be chic, she says. I once threw a book at my mother, but I didn't mean to actually hit her with it. When she tells people the story she makes it sound like it was a Russian brick of a novel, but really it was just a slim poetry collection by Henrik Nordbrandt. Seadragon, I believe. Imagine that, attacked by a dragon, my mother says when I point this out.

*

My father wakes me up the next morning. Grethe's sick, he says. I look at the clock, it's a little past ten. I groan. It's the middle of the night, I say. I have a wedding at two, my father says. His forehead is wrinkled with worry. No, I say, just no. Grethe is the soloist at his church. You have such a lovely voice, he says. No, I say, I have a hangover. You know all the hymns inside out, he says, you sing like an angel.

Isn't there some kind of musical temp agency you can call, I ask, turning over in bed. My father starts talking about my time in the church choir. I say it's strange that my broken heart has inspired so many people to scream yes to one another in churches lately. I fall back asleep. A few minutes later, my father comes in with a cup of coffee and two pieces of toast. His wife follows behind, laying a black dress and a hymnal on the bed. You're manipulating me, I say. Yes, my father says. Why can't you be an engineer like all the normal fathers, I say. Can't you sing, I say, looking at my father's wife. No, my father says, she's the organist. What's wrong with multi-tasking, I say, think of Elton John. I lie down again and look up at the ceiling. I've been abandoned, I say, and you're making a mockery of my broken heart. No, my father says, we're making a wedding happen. He looks at his wife. It's just one wedding, she says. I'm going to have to find another place to live, I say. My father's wife nods. I sit up in the bed. How fine it is to cooooome along, I holler out across the room. My father's wife gets her portable keyboard and sits at the edge of my bed. She plays a few chords. Not everything revolves around you, she says. I sing the first two verses. She smiles at me and says we can make fried pork belly with parsley sauce for dinner. I get to the fourth verse. How sad it is that we must part, I sing, and I start to cry. There there, my father's wife says, I'm sure you'll get married plenty of times. My father stands in the doorway with a satisfied look on his face. This'll be fun, he says.

*

My doctor looks serious today. He says that trust is important, that it's a precondition to any relationship. I want to talk to you, my doctor says, but it seems like you always avoid the very subjects that have perhaps caused you to come here. I just suffer from free-floating associations, I say. It's important to trust your doctor, my doctor says. I nod. I think of the British doctor Harold Shipman, who systematically murdered his patients. Trust, my doctor says, looking right at me. I tell my doctor to consider the case of Dr. Struensee. He was just a physician, but he managed to seduce Queen Caroline Mathilde, and, as if that weren't enough, he took control of the whole kingdom after declaring Christian VII insane. My doctor looks at me. He looks tired. His silence starts to make me feel crazy. I decide to extend an olive branch. But doctors are only human, I say. He nods. I look at my doctor. I wish he would move just one single muscle in his face. I say that there are, of course, less turbulent figures out there, and I mention the poet Emil Aarestrup, who also worked as a country doctor. Hold me tighter with your round arms, I say. My doctor looks nervous. It's a quotation, I say quickly, from a poem called Angst. My doctor looks relieved. I say that the imperatives work well, the nature symbolism less well, and that the slight tonal break in the second verse suggests a general fragility, that all things are subject to decay. I clap out the meter for him. You can't even rely on rhythm, I say. He suggests that I may have strayed off topic. I look out the window and join him in silence. My doctor clears his throat and says my name. He seems shocked when he notices I'm crying. He leaps up from his chair and runs to the sink and grabs three packs of Kleenex while saying my name again and again. He puts them in a pile in front of me and says that he's got more in the drawer. For a split second, my doctor reminds me of all the men I've ever known. He probably always carries an umbrella in case of rain, possibly even two in case the first one breaks. He shifts uneasily in his chair and stares helplessly at the tissues, and I suspect that he'd like to invent a medication for the prevention of female tears. He asks if I want a glass of water. I say no thanks, and he finds a little plastic cup and turns on the faucet. My doctor hands me the cup and tells me there's more where that came from. There are light strands at the end of the tunnel, he says. I look out the window. Leaves fly through the air, drawn by the wind, the shattered color palettes of a restless painter. You're probably right, I say, folding one of the tissues into a paper airplane. I aim for his nose, and it flies off over the table.

Monologues of a Seahorse V

Inside my belly button is a circus ring where we all walk in circles. We follow each other in little processions, the elephants in front, followed by the sea lions, the magicians with their top hats full of rabbits, the acrobats doing daredevil leaps, and the clowns throwing pies at each other while they laugh their piercing laughter. The tightrope walker walks on stilts across a wire stretched through the air above. We wander the ring to rounds of applause and trembling silences. Surrounding the circus ring is a tent, and surrounding the tent is a world, but we've stopped believing in it. All attempts to escape are futile, and the elephants sigh, the sea lions cry, the clowns sob, the tightrope walker falls, and the rabbits scratch each other's eyes out. But still we walk around and around mechanically, little bubbles of people and animals who've accepted defeat without even putting up a fight. If someone saw us from above, we'd look like miniature dolls grasping at one another with words and sentences and reaching hands, our eyes wide and our arms extended. We misunderstand one another, sometimes on purpose, sometimes out of habit, occasionally as a subtle act of revenge, but most of the time because our misunderstandings are all we have. We tell ourselves that we can form relationships, and we dream that people are irreplaceable. The few times we actually do forget the existence of loneliness, we become so ecstatically happy that we call it love, even though the closest we can come to love is the possibility of meeting a person who periodically makes us doubt our aloneness. Our only hope lies in brief flashes of fleeting intimacy, which don't replace our loneliness but can, at best, subsist alongside it. Then we become euphoric and say yes to one another in churches, live side by side in our treadmills, leaving parallel footprints across the globe. Then we feel a creeping sensation that it's an illusion, because inside our belly buttons there is a circus ring, but before there was a belly button there was an umbilical cord, and once it gets cut it's never possible for us to be one with another person. The memory of closeness is lodged in our belly buttons, and we never truly grasp that we've been severed from everyone else. In our despair we procreate, longing to be connected with a living thing, only to be separated from these beings by a single clip of the scissors. And from that moment on we'll never be as close again, and we'll never be able to fully accept it, and suddenly our loneliness doubles. We go back to the circus ring in resignation, and slowly it dawns on us that all things are bounded by themselves. We walk in circles, think in circles, talk in circles, the words we speak are vinyl records spinning, we live on a round planet, look at round things with our round eyes in our round faces. We're enduring armies of one, marching around in circus rings with phosphorescent haloes of loneliness following us everywhere we go.

MY FATHER HAS hung a red knitted stocking at the foot of my bed. When I open my eyes, a big chocolate Santa is poking its head out of the stocking and smiling at me. I stare back at its ecstatic chocolate face and wake with a start. I take it with me into the kitchen and stand it up beside the coffee machine. It watches me as I light a cigarette, pour coffee into the filter, and put two slices of bread in the toaster. I drill a little hole through its chocolate mouth with a fork and stick a cigarette between its lips. We smoke in silence. My father comes into the kitchen and smiles with delight. You two seem to be getting along well, he says, pointing at the chocolate man. My father's hair is disheveled and he looks small in his baggy pajamas. He says he thinks he heard something heavy fall down the chimney last night. Thump, he says, and he puts his coffee cup down hard on the table. Coffee sloshes out, forming a little brown puddle. And Rudolph's bells were ringing up on the roof, my father says. He hums a few bars of Rudolph the Red-Nosed Reindeer. I drop a tablet into a glass of water and mumble something about how I was out late with Mulle last night so I must've missed it. The Santa smiles ecstatically. Bubbles rise to the surface of the water. My father talks about how we could make candied desserts together this afternoon. He lights his pipe and says there's a Christmas market at the church where we could set up a booth. My temples throb. My father smiles. The Santa laughs and smokes. It looks evil. My father's wife comes into the kitchen. She looks from me to my father to the Santa in the middle. I take the cigarette out from between Santa's lips and light it for myself. It tastes slightly chocolatey. My father's wife opens the window and removes charred slices of bread from the toaster. Whoops, my father says, we're always forgetting those. She nods. Santa laughs soundlessly, a hole running straight through his skull. I lean on the windowsill and try to catch snowflakes in my smoke rings. My father says I'm doing it all wrong. You've got to account for the direction of the wind, he says, coming to my side. We lean out the window and blow smoke rings into the sunrise. Look here, like this, he says, and he blows a perfectly formed circle which wraps around a snowflake. It reminds me of the time he taught me to skip stones on the North Sea when I was little. My father's wife starts scraping the black off of the bread. We make a competition to see who can catch the most snowflakes. My father wins 5–2. Why do you always have to win, I say, and I bite Santa's head off. I feel nauseous. My father looks pleased, and he asks me if it tastes good. It tastes like Santa bought the cheapest chocolate he could find at Aldi. I nod. When my father goes to take a shower a little later, I throw up in the trash can. There are big brown clumps in my vomit. I look over at the decapitated chocolate body. My father's wife hands me a glass of water.

*

It's afternoon by the time I hear my father open the door to the living room. He comes in and smiles at me as he puts two rolls of marzipan and a plate of dark chocolate on the table. I'm sitting in his recliner watching Dr. Quinn, Medicine Woman and eating pizza. A little gypsy boy has shown up in Doctor Quinn's town. He's sad and he can't speak and everyone wants to run him out of town because his mother worked as a prostitute in the local saloon before she died. Michaela discovers that he's good at drawing and eventually he gets into an art academy, but in the meantime she tracks down his estranged father and manages to convince him to take responsibility for the boy. I cry a little when they reunite on a train-station platform. Thank goodness for Doctor Mike, I say to my father. He looks shocked, and he brings me a paper towel. You seem to be happy with your doctor, my father says. There's no one like Doctor Mike, I say. It's just a TV show, my father says, patting me on the head. He talks about the importance of distinguishing fact from fiction. My father goes to get some food coloring from the kitchen, and when he comes back he's wearing a Santa hat. Now it's confection time, he says, passing me a pale, pasty clump in the shape of a sausage. He talks about the Salvation Army and how the homeless have a tough time around Christmas from the kitchen as he melts chocolate in a double boiler. I can't bear the sight of the pale marzipan. It's the same color as my thighs in wintertime, I say to my father. I spray green food coloring onto the pasty clump and sculpt some little marzipan Christmas trees. My father says they're going to turn out beautifully, and he asks what I've been up to today. I say that I called my ex-girlfriend and then hung up on her five times. Shouldn't you be thinking about your thesis instead, my father says. I say that it's important to stay up to date, and that I could deduce from the background noise that she was walking around town. He says that she might need a little space, that I can always come by the church if I'm bored. I ask my father if he thinks she's met someone else. She'll never find anyone as sweet as you, he says, mussing up my hair. My father asks me if I've considered looking for a new partner, he says sometimes the best thing is to start afresh. You'd know all about that, I say. My father sprinkles candied violets on top of my Christmas trees. The important thing is to find someone you can really talk to, my father says, somehow who's a good listener. I make a marzipan sculpture of my doctor. I dip the head into the melted chocolate to give him dark hair, and I stick two little tips of almonds in for eyes. I dip the almond tips in green food coloring. Is that me, my father asks, pointing at my marzipan man. I nod, and I dab a bit of the chocolate off of his head to make a bald spot, and I add a bit more marzipan to his belly. The gravel crunches outside, and I see my mother biking down the driveway. She smiles and waves. So much for a peaceful Christmas, I say. My father nods.

*

My mother comes into the living room and says she just wanted to know whether I'd made an appointment with my academic advisor. I say that I've tried to call five times but I couldn't get through. The Christmas bustle, I say, people go berserk. My mother eats a few of our marzipan trees. Those are for the homeless, my father says. My mother says that she feels sorry for the homeless, truly sorry, but that you have to remember that they don't have any fixed expenses. I eat the misshapen pieces of marzipan, and I make them a little uneven on purpose. These just won't do at the Christmas market, I say to my father, and furthermore, I'm now homeless myself. All this whining, my mother says, don't you ever get tired of listening to yourself. My mother says I need to watch out or I'll end up an overweight social outcast who never finished her education. Your ex-wife is implying that I'm fat, I say to my father. He looks confused. My mother bites my marzipan man's head off. You're eating dad, I scream, you're making me fatherless, are you insane. We'll just make another one, my father says. You're spoiling her, my mother says as she chews my father's head. I can hear his eyes crunch between her teeth. Cannibal, I hiss. You've always spoiled her, my mother says. We're just trying to enjoy Christmas, my father says. If it weren't for me she wouldn't be able to make it through that door today, my mother says, if I hadn't set some boundaries when she was a child she would've ended up at fat camp. You were decidedly overweight, my mother says, looking at me. Be careful darling, she says, you tend toward corpulence. She snatches the piece of marzipan I'm about to eat and puts it in her mouth. You were a little plump, that's all, my father says, patting me on the head. And you were always so happy when you got to eat chocolate, my father says, looking happy himself. So you stuffed her with candy every time she whined, just because you wanted to see her smile, my mother says. My father looks slightly ashamed. Good lord, he says, Christmas only comes once a year.

*

There's a Christmas market in The Old Town. Mulle pushes her grandmother's wheelchair. The old lady sits, wrapped in a knitted shawl, watching a reconstruction of her youth through a pair of yellow-tinted glasses. She has a fur hat on and her hands are buried in a muff. You look like Misse and Aunt Møhge, I say to Mulle and her grandmother. It's the priest's daughter, Mulle's grandmother shouts. I take her hand and pat her fur hat. She likes laaaadies, Mulle's grandmother shouts to Mulle while pointing at me. Mulle nods. They say that's the fashion these days, Mulle's grandmother says, scowling as she says the word fashion. That's right, I say, it's crazy what you have to do to stay in style. Mulle's grandmother asks me how I'm doing. My girlfriend kicked me out, I yell into her hearing aid. That's what happens when you don't tie the knot, Mulle's grandmother screams, a bird in the hand is worth ten on the roof. I hate birds, I say. I can't understand why no one wants you, Mulle's grandmother says, you were always such a sweet girl. I nod. You sat at my bedside in the hospital and sang hymns for me when I got my new hip, Mulle's grandmother says. This is one of her favorite stories. True, she never quite recovered from her time in church choir, Mulle says. We buy a glass of mulled wine for Mulle's grandmother and roll her over to a display of animated elves. The red steam gives her glasses a pink sheen. Christmas is starting to get on my nerves, I say, decorations are covering every surface of the parsonage, and my evil stepmother plays Christmas music all day long. Your father's a wonderful man, Mulle's grandmother shouts as she rocks in time to Skinnamarink, which one of the elves is playing on the accordion. It's about time for you to meet someone new, Mulle says. I say that I'm nowhere near ready for that. You should find a man next time, Mulle's grandmother shouts. Times have changed, Grandma, Mulle says. Mulle's grandmother snorts. Just make sure he's not black, Mulle's grandmother says, that'd be even worse. Mulle turns off her hearing aid and puts a blanket around her. Maybe I'm just meant to be alone, I say, some people aren't suited to coupledom. The problem with you young people is that you don't give things a chance, Mulle's grandmother screams, you're too busy with your wantonness. She talks about Mulle's grandfather, who died years ago. He reminds me of the priest, she says. How long does it take to move on, I ask Mulle's grandmother as I pass her a little twist of fried dough. It's too soft, Mulle says, snatching the twist away, it'll get stuck in her dentures. Give it back, Mulle's grandmother shouts. A Santa Claus stops and looks at us with reproach. Mulle's grandmother takes her hands out of her muff and waves at him flamboyantly. She spits her dentures into my hand and takes a bite of the twist. Mulle's grandmother says that she thinks of her husband every day, but that she's capable of thinking of other things too. Like the priest, for example, Mulle says. Insolent girl, Mulle's grandmother says as she takes another bite of the twist. I tell Mulle that I'm considering fleeing the country. I'm going back to India, I say. Mulle's grandmother has fallen asleep by the time dusk settles over The Old Town. When I'm about to bike back home, she wakes with a start and hands me a cookie tin. These are for the priest, Mulle's grandmother says with a toothless smile, and I trade her the dentures in my pocket for a tin of butter cookies.

*

I ask my doctor if some people are just chemically incompatible with coupledom, and if you can have a greater or lesser degree of talent at the practice of love. He says that there are, of course, asexual people out there, but that it's no longer considered a psychological dysfunction. Asexuality really isn't the issue here, I say, and if that's the scale we're using then I'm probably more on the nymphomaniac side of things. My doctor tells me that it's very normal to deny one's asexuality, not least because there's so little research on the subject, and that asexual people often feel excluded from society at large. He says that the phenomenon has also been observed in various mammals, horses, goats, and rabbits, among others. As I said, I don't think I'm asexual, I say. He says that it's actually incredibly difficult to detect asexuality, because studies show that animals without a libido have the same hormone levels as their sexually active brethren. He rests his hands on the table and clasps them together. He clears his throat and says that we seem to have strayed from the subject of relationships. He goes on a little about the importance of trust and the vital role of openness. But I talk all the time, I say, I feel like a pink Duracell Bunny. The way in which one talks is also of some importance, my doctor says cautiously, fiddling with the hole puncher on the table. I ask him if he gets extra vacation days for taking on especially annoying patients like myself, or perhaps a tax deduction. He clears his throat and says he knows I'm going through a hard time right now. I ask if doctors love their patients no matter what. Some of them, he says with a faint smile.

*

I wake up with a headache. I don't recognize the room. I take a look around and then promptly throw up. An officer opens the door and hands me a glass of water. Am I under arrest, I groan. You'll have to pay for the window panes, he says, but we don't send people to jail for disorderly conduct. I don't feel so good, I must've been really drunk, I say. He nods. I've been abandoned, I say. He asks if there's anyone he can call for me. I empty the glass of water. My parents pick me up at the police station twenty minutes later. I stand at the counter and watch them through the window. The sun slices into my eyes, it feels like torture. My mother traipses across the frozen puddles in high heels. Have you lost your mind, my mother says as the door opens. I never asked to be born into this world, I say, it's your fault. My father looks worried and takes a slight step back. I look down at the ground. Silly girl, my father says. He hands me a bag with a bottle of mineral water, some headache medicine, and a pack of cigarettes. My mother tears the cigarettes from my hand and takes one out. My father lights it. Maybe somebody spiked my drink, I say. Oh shut up, my mother says. My father clears his throat. He says it's important to stand tall in the face of adversity. Oh shut up, my mother says, pointing at me, she has the spine of an earthworm. Good lord, my father says, it's not like she killed somebody. Very true, I say. Were you out with Mulle last night, my mother asks. Spin doctors always vacate the premises before things get messy, I say. An elderly officer tells my parents that I won't be charged with vandalism as long as I'm willing to pay a fine. My father writes a check. I throw up in a trash can. My mother lights another cigarette. My father says we don't need to mention any of this again. Oh shut up, my mother says, we'll be discussing this at length. It's also possible to talk too much, my father says. No it's not, my mother says. She's just sad, my father says. I nod and lay my head on his shoulder. You've lost your mind, and you're a whiner, my mother hisses. I'm lonely, I say, why did she leave me. One can only guess, my mother says. The officer comes back with a receipt. You'd better keep an eye on the young lady, he says, pointing at me, she almost tore this place apart last night. Oh shut up, my mother says, there's nothing wrong with my daughter, she's just sad. That doesn't give her the right to lash out at our employees, the officer says. Maybe it does, my father says. My mother marches back to the car, her handbag swinging at her side. The sun hits the snow on her red hat and it looks like her hair is full of light.

*

India, my doctor says. I nod. I hate Christmas, I say, and I'm not coming back until the local authorities have removed every single elf from public spaces. It's an act of protest, I say to my doctor. He prepares the needle. I detect a certain glee in his eyes and feel a pang of dread. He tells me about a research project he once took part in. It was a lot of fun, he says, sounding genuinely happy that he stabbed all those mice. I say that fun may not be the right word. An image pops into my mind which I'd prefer to have gone without. I picture a younger version of him, surrounded by dead mice, the same subtly triumphant look on his face. But the mice weren't easy to work with, he tells me. They're resistant to almost everything, with makes them almost impossible to kill. He looks a little disappointed. He picks up the needle again. This shouldn't hurt, he says, rolling a cotton ball between his fingers and whistling gently. I think of blood. He works quickly, focused, and I'm annoyed by how beautiful his hands are. Suddenly I know just what he looked like as a seven-year-old boy playing with Lego bricks. Concentrated, mildly autistic, totally detached from the world. He looks up at me as if he's just rediscovered my existence, and he smiles an intimate smile as the needle draws near my shoulder. I think of sharp objects, the time an Italian lady hit me with a dart in Florence, flat-headed pushpins pointing up from the floorboards, wasps, rusty nails sticking out of walls. He brushes my hair away from my shoulder. Of course he was right, it doesn't hurt, but I scream unrestrainedly nonetheless for the sake of atmosphere. I can't stand people who are right. But not even my theatrics can ruffle his steady hands. Merry Christmas and happy travels, he says as I disappear into the falling snow.

*

A few days later I'm sitting on my father's sofa beneath a blanket. My father's wife has bundled me up in scarves and I can barely breathe. I'm in the midst of a coughing fit when my mother calls. Are you sick, my mother says. She sounds threatening. No, I whisper, though I can barely speak. My mother starts scolding me, she always gets mad at me when I'm sick. She talks about warm clothes, healthy eating, half an hour of exercise every day, and she has several theories about the effects of stress. You've been burning the candle at both ends, she yells. I cough and gasp for air. You sound like a man, my mother screams, with all your whining and your unhealthy living, haven't I told you about this before. Yes, I whisper. My mother says she's going to give me a new coat. It'll be ugly and warm and you're never going to take it off, she yells. Even in the summer, I whisper. Yes, she thunders, and you're going to use your asthma spray and quit smoking and go to bed at a decent hour. You need to get well, my mother screams, you need to get well and be happy. I need to go to the doctor, I whisper. No, my mother yells, you're totally obsessed with that doctor, a mother can sense these things. My head hurts, and I hold the phone as far away as possible. My father comes into the living room. I pull the blanket over my head and hand him the phone. Yes, she's sick, my father says. Not all that much, he says after a while, and only menthols. I can hear the sound of my mother's voice from under the blanket. My temples are pounding and my body is damp with sweat. Good lord, my father says. I look over the edge of the blanket. My father has the television on and he's watching a hockey game on mute. Someone scores, and my father looks happy. A bunch of men on skates embrace one another and laugh. Over the next few minutes my father makes vague noises of agreement at periodic intervals until at last he says goodbye. She's just worried about you, my father says. Mamma's gonna make all your nightmares come true, Mamma's gonna put all her fears into you, he sings softly as he turns up the volume of the hockey game.

Monologues of a Seahorse VI

Inside my mouth is a stalactite-covered cavern, a dark red expanse with ivory columns lining the chambers where teenagers dance as if their lives depend on it. This is where I remember your tastes, our tongues dancing like wet sea monsters as we meld together. We are a heap of preschool children playing, a ball of yarn, a head of braids in disarray, we're dusty computer cables, we're spaghetti stuck together in a big clump of carbohydrates. You who taste slightly salty, and you with your aftertaste of lavender. And you chewing licorice-flavored gum, and you with your spicy sausage. Here you all are with your lips, their curvatures, the taste buds on your tongues, their little dots leading to your uvulas, behind which is a treasure chest where I put your smiles for safekeeping. Your lips in their countless formations, the corners of your mouths, your muscle contractions. And the countless things that flow from your smiles, the concurrent movements that attend them. You, when you looked down, the fold of your eyelids, your thin skin is a movie screen and the fine pink lines of your veins are the branches of a tree in the botanical gardens. And you with your crow's feet pointing in five different directions, drawing patterns upon your face, long arcing arabesques in your skin. And you with your dimples slowly appearing, they are the army of insects that sits on my yellow dress as the first drops start to fall from a summer storm, and after, the puddles I want to swim around in. I see your smiles before me in their countless poses, and I am bewitched and bewildered and besotted. I see them everywhere, your phantom smiles. I see them strung up on lampposts at election time, the candidates smile and smile, but it is your smiles I see, hanging in the trees like upside-down cherries, swaying from the telephone lines, your smiles, hung up with clips and clothespins and blowing in the wind. There are real smiles and fake smiles, each reserved for a different occasion, and they can be combined, your smiles, they can flow into one another, glide across other expressions, replace each other, and coexist. I open my treasure chest from behind your uvulas and I am blinded by your smiles, they shimmer back at me, and I am gripped with panic at the thought that your smiles might disappear. So I will hoard them in all their permutations, and I will become a sculptor and mold your smiles in clay, I will cast your smiles in bronze and put them up on exhibition. With a stick I will draw your smiles on sandy beaches, carve them into trees with a rusty pocket knife, tattoo them onto my arms like a sailor, until at last they engulf me.

I'M OUT AT a bar with Mulle one night. Suddenly I see my doctor sitting at a table over in the corner. Let's sit over here, I say to Mulle, weaving my way to a nearby table. I move a big floor plant a little so it blocks my face. Who are you hiding from, Mulle asks. The world, I say. My doctor is with a group of men his age, it sounds like they're his colleagues. They talk and laugh, something about eye operations and a jittery surgeon they know. There's something about men in their mid-thirties that reminds me of pubescent boys. Just like back then, they speak in raucous voices about everything except what's actually on their minds. They attempt to walk the line between a careless youthfulness and an enviable worldliness which mustn't tend toward the fatherly. When Mulle stands up to get a gin and tonic they all go silent. I watch through the leaves of the plant. Mulle is beautiful. Today her long red hair looks like lava flowing down her back. The doctors stare at the volcano as it passes them by. One of them lifts an eyebrow and smiles at her, but it's a smile that no longer believes even in itself. They all try to look a little younger than they are without being obvious about it. They pretend that they don't have to be home by a certain hour, and that they don't have to go back to work on Monday. But there's a weariness in their faces which won't be concealed. They don't know that their true attraction lies not in these exertions, but rather in their phosphorescent longing, their yearning for something else. Not something bigger or something more beautiful, just something other than that which has befallen them. They're happy, they love their wives, and they especially love their children. They have no regrets, but that's precisely why they can't understand this all-consuming boredom, this baffling friction, which shouldn't be there in the first place, but is so pervasive that its excess energies beam out of their eyes and their mouths and skip after their bodies like shadows. Mulle puts two beers down in front of us. Cheers, she shouts, raising her glass to the table in the corner. As if on cue, they straighten their backs and lift their glasses and smile, all at once and in more or less the same fashion, slightly stunned, like they've just woken up. I shrink down a little. Looks like a table of midlife crises, Mulle whispers. They're everywhere, I say, they're little neon lights illuminating the globe. They sit in bars across the world, either alone or in groups, but always with the same aimless stare. Mulle asks me whether we're trying to have fun or conduct humanistic field research. I start talking about the existential conditions of life. The melancholy, Mulle, I say, the meaninglessness. Let's play dice, she says. She puts two leather cups on the table.

*

I drop a die on the floor and crawl under the table to fetch it. I overhear fragments of the doctors' sentences. Though I assume that they're carrying on a conversation, it sounds like they're all wailing. Not at one another or anyone in particular, just wailing deafeningly into space. Most of them are wailing because they're married and have children and feel suffocated by a formulaic happiness. And the other ones, the ones who always want to hit the next bar, they wail because they feel suffocated by an equally formulaic freedom. Mulle and I harbor a different desperation and a different kind of wail. Because we haven't yet made any commitments that can't be rescinded, all our potential bad choices are lined up before us, awaiting their enactment. We sense their constant presence, but our regrets are still abstractions, and so our angst is harder to identify. Time still absolves us, but we know we're getting older even if we can't feel it. The signs aren't obvious, they can't yet be read upon our bodies, but very soon we'll no longer be the objects of their gazes, and our youth will no longer pardon us. I realize how drunk I'm getting when I crawl back onto my chair and the room spins. I part the leaves of the plant so I can see the corner table. Mulle asks if I've become a private detective, and she says it'd probably pay better than the jobs I can get with my humanities degree. I watch my doctor through the plant. He seems slightly more reserved than the others, with a searching expression that makes me want to be found. I think about how he probably sat there ten years ago, possibly in the very same chair; but the becoming gauze of melancholy that surrounds him must have grown over time. He thrums his fingers on the table and fiddles with the ashtray, as if waiting for something to happen without quite knowing what it should be. A pair of fives, Mulle says, you're the worst person I know at dice.

*

As I bike home to the parsonage it smells like spring, even though it's a little too early. All the tears we've cried through life, they vanish on a spring day, I sing. I think about the little gathering at the corner table, now dispersed into the world. I picture them walking around in their apartments with a sensation of being in a film they've seen before. They look at their furniture and the pictures on their walls and wonder how they wound up here. And they look at the people they married. They contemplate how their body language has changed with time. They think about how the touch between themselves and their spouses has become such a natural extension of their own bodies that it can no longer be considered touch, but something so indifferent that it's more akin to a series of random collisions. I wobble a little on my bike and find my balance again. But now the room's gone silent and I'm lost for words, I sing. A film starts to play in my head, and I envision their lives. Maybe I should be a director, I say to a birch tree as I ride past it. The leaves blow in the wind and it seems to nod back at me. I zoom in on everyone in their mid-thirties. They all talk about their children with the same worry and love, they nurture them and comfort them and take them to the swimming pool. Their children's babbling elicits smiles and affectionate looks across their kitchens. Their eyes meet over layer cakes topped with three candles and they feel the warmth and think of themselves as a love machine, a rumbling motor kept alive by the people they've created. They bring their children teddy bears and glasses of milk at night and they pull out loose teeth. They pick up brightly colored puzzle pieces from their floors with simultaneous movements and they pack lunch boxes in unison. They know that they love their partners, and that they love them in the same way they draw breath, unthinkingly and out of necessity. I try to light a cigarette while riding my bike. The second after I finally get it lit, I fall off. I stay on the ground for a while playing dead, but since there's no one around I get up again. Back in the saddle, I say in a deep voice. And I think of my father. I set a new scene. Now they're over for dinner with another couple. They're only sporadically interested in their friends' children, but they like it when they can contribute stories and comparable anecdotes about their own. They look at each other across the table and say we and us and feel a reassuring sense of communion, something meaningful, worth insisting upon, something made manifest by the words themselves. They speak in gentle voices, and the names associated with these stories, which are interesting only to the parents, are interchangeable and inconsequential, because the remarkable thing is their voices. They speak in the same cadence as all parents who've ever existed. They sound like they're sighing all the time, both when they speak and when they listen, both when they're sighing and when they're not sighing. They tell each other that the first three years are the hardest, but after the first three years they'll have exactly the same conversation, merely extending the time frame until their children go to school, and then onward to puberty, until, in a final drawn-out surrender, they'll concede that things might go back to normal when the kids move out. In a way it's touching how they always talk as if something will come back, I say to a cat, who stops and looks up at me while I park my bike outside the parsonage. As if there were a passion that will resurrect itself in the course of time, I say, stroking its fur. The cat seems interested in what I have to say. It's fascinating how they can convince themselves that they'll wake up one morning and everything will be the way it was before. How can they be sure that the desire that will someday stir again will necessarily be directed toward the people they're married to, I ask. It's a conviction that wavers between awe-inspiring stupidity and immeasurable beauty, I say to the cat. It has orange fur and looks a bit like Garfield. If Mulle were a cat, she'd look just like you, I say. When I get into the kitchen I see a plate covered in tinfoil which my father and his wife have left out for me. It's lasagna and bean salad. I take the lasagna out to the garden and sit down beside Garfield. Suddenly I'm touched by how sweet my father and his wife are. They always think of me, I say to Garfield. I sway back inside and kneel outside their bedroom door. I'm sure you know it deep down, even though I'm lost for words, I sing through the keyhole. My father opens the door in his pajamas. I try to whistle the solo, but I can tell it works better when Anne Linnet plays it on guitar. Goodnight, my father says.

*

The next day I wake up early and make breakfast for my father and his wife. Bacon and eggs and little American pancakes with syrup. Looks like someone has a guilty conscience, my father's wife says. I'm sorry I woke you up last night, I say. She laughs. It's already forgotten, my father says, looking at the mountain of bacon piled on his plate. What I like best about my father's wife is her hoarse laughter. She sounds like a rock star who's just returned from a world tour. You can always start a bed-and-breakfast if all else fails, she says. All else has failed, I say. As my father walks over to the church, the idea slowly takes hold of me. I tell my father's wife that I haven't really started on my thesis. Maybe it's not what you really want, she says. My father's wife talks about the old barn they never use. I'm going to start a breakfast restaurant, I say, that's my new goal in life. My father's wife says that's always been a dream of hers. She gets some colored pencils and a notepad, and we draw sketches of the restaurant. Little round tables and a small wardrobe. She draws a massive grand piano in the corner. I draw bookshelves on the other side. You can use our kitchen to make food for the guests, my father's wife says. We arrange sheets of paper on the floor and tape them together so we can crawl around in the restaurant. A good atmosphere is essential, my father's wife says, and I draw vases with sunflowers on the tables. She adds some candles and checkered curtains. I draw some palms on the floor and a little fountain in the middle of the room. My father's wife wrinkles her forehead when she sees my fountain. Is it the electricity bill, I ask. She says that it's important to stick to one style so it doesn't get too chaotic. Let's go with the baroque, I say, and I turn the fountain into a sculpture of a chubby angel with a benevolent smile. My father's wife draws little flourishes on the window frames and adorns the curtains with elaborate lace patterns. We need vanitas symbols, I say. We put some skulls on the shelves as bookends. My mother can stand off in the corner and blow soap bubbles over the guests, I say, that ought to keep her out of the way. We write down some ideas for the menu. Baroque-brunch, Leonora Christina–croissants, and Kingo-cakes. And no alcohol, I say, people can't handle it. You can play for the guests, I say to my father's wife, it'll be so nice. We get her portable keyboard and make a provisional playlist. We'll open with Chrysillis, to set the tone, I say. Draw nigh, o' faithful heart, and lend me your ear, as I for you do sing, we sing. And the guests will wait in long lines to get in, I say, the congregation can come right over to me after my dad has preached them hungry, it's familial synergy. Café Chrysillis, says my father's wife.

*

One morning the doorbell rings, and my father answers the door. My mother has a dead fox around her neck, which she hangs on a hook. It's time to shake things up around here, she says as she gives me a hug. I have a headache. Have you been out drinking again, my mother asks. It's Mulle's fault, I say, that girl knows no restraint. We sit down at the table, and I ask my father to order a pizza. Number sixteen with extra cheese and bacon, he says, looking at me. I nod. My father heads for the phone, but my mother blocks his path. I brought a salad, she says, with shredded apples and raisins. Why, my father asks. You've got to change your mindset, she says, it's about lifestyle. She points at him. And we need to stand together as parents, my mother says, she's your daughter too, so you need to start acting like a father. My father clears his throat. All right then, let's give the salad a try, my father says, and he gets some plates and forks from the kitchen. My mother has found a number for an academic advisor. How's your thesis coming along, she says. You're so result-oriented, I say, it's about the process. I talk about the type of parent who puts too much pressure on their children. We don't need no education, we don't need no thought control, I sing. My father drums the rhythm on the table with his fork. My mother says that I'd better finish my thesis. What exactly have you been doing with yourself for the past six months, she asks. I look over to the corner of the living room where my father's wife and I built a miniature version of our breakfast restaurant. We found an old doll house at a flea market and bought tiny furniture for our café. I look at my father. He clears his throat. I've read through some of Dad's sermons, I say. My father looks confused for a moment, but then he nods in agreement. It's relevant to her studies, he says. You could become a copyeditor, my father says to me with smile. It's safe to assume that you two have just been playing cards and listening to the radio, my mother says. She's got to get back in the saddle, my father mumbles, everything takes time. I will not allow my daughter to become one of those eternal students who never finish their education, my mother says. She looks at my father, and then she looks at me. I've found an apartment, my mother says, one of my colleagues is renting it out and it's perfect for you, darling. Okay, I say. Party's over, my mother says. My father looks a little sad. My mother rolls her eyes and puts her hand on his arm. She can't keep living with you for the rest of her life, my mother says, she's an adult. It would've been fun though, my father says. It's a stone's throw from the pedestrian street, you'll love it, my mother says with a smile.

*

I can always tell when it's my mother ringing the doorbell. She's standing outside with her arms full of flowers. There are five Danish flags lodged down into the bouquet. Congratulations on your new apartment, she says as she hands me the flowers. Thanks, I say, stepping out of her way. My mother brought along some portraits of herself. The walls are so bare in here, she says. A few of the portraits were taken for her work. She's pictured standing next to a house, a wild smile on her face. Beside her is a sign that says for sale in capital letters. She shows me some childhood pictures with her in a purple dress and long black braids. Don't we look so much alike, darling, she says, tugging on my ponytail. She finds a magnet and hangs her wedding photo up on the refrigerator. My mother and her husband are smiling in front of the church. My father stands off to the side, looking slightly confused. My mother has also enlarged a photo of herself as a baby, which she's put into an old golden frame. She walks around hanging the photographs on the walls with little pushpins. Now I can really keep an eye on you, she says, laughing. I was so cute, my mother says, putting the baby photo in the middle of an empty bookshelf. Where are all your books, she asks. I say that my crazy ex-girlfriend is holding them hostage. You haven't gone to get them yet, have you, she asks. I shake my head. You're just like your father, she says, you never get anything done. I say it's problematic that she always compares me to a person she chose to divorce. She says that my father is all right, a magnificent cook and very helpful. She tells me that he'll help me pick up the books. I say that I can't bring myself to go into the old apartment, that I can't handle seeing my ex-girlfriend. Your father will help you and it'll be fine, she says, he's got a direct line to you-know-who. She points up at the ceiling. It smells like smoke in here, my mother says. I move some empty gin bottles so I can open the window. My mother can't stand it when I say that she reminds me of my grandmother, which is why I periodically bring it to her attention. You remind me of Grandma, I say, you're so nosy. Grandma's dead, she says, and I'm not. The flags in the bouquet flutter gently in the breeze. I tell my mother that I'm happy she's not dead, and I worry that it may be the sweetest thing I've ever said to her.

*

I sit on a bench in the corner of the cemetery and wait for my father. I watch a group of people dressed in black as they walk in a line, my father leading the way. Two young women embrace as the procession gathers around a burial plot and splits into smaller groups. After a while the crowd dissolves and only one middle-aged woman remains, staring at the grave. My father comes out of the church office in his own clothes. He waves to me as he walks toward the bench. Then Mulle's grandmother appears, driving after him in her electric wheelchair. She blocks his path and grabs him by the hand. She holds it firmly between her hands and smiles toothlessly up at him. He points over at me, and I wave to them. You'd better watch out, I say when he finally tears himself away, Mulle's grandmother's on the warpath, after fourteen years as a widow I think she's ready to move on. My father looks confused, then scared. You've got to get back in the saddle, I say. I put my arm around his shoulder and we walk to the car. My father always looks somber after holding a funeral. He's rented a van and found some old moving boxes, he doesn't think my books can fit in the Toyota. My father adjusts the side-view mirror and puts on a David Bowie CD. When we pull up in front her apartment, I feel like I can't go in after all. We'll just get the boxes and go, my father says. Maybe I don't actually need those books, I say, when you get down to it they're just pieces of paper covered in little black letters. He turns the music down and looks at me. We need to support our public institutions, I say, and I talk about the outstanding selection of books in the country's libraries. He gets out of the car and walks off toward a grocery store. He comes back a little later with a bag of chocolate drops. We eat them in silence. It'll be fine, he says, we'll just get the boxes and go. We could also just not get the boxes and go, I say. He clears his throat. Try not to make a scene, he says, tousling my hair. What if she's found some hideous lover with a deformed face, I say, and what if that mutant is up there reading my books right now. Then we'll just get the boxes and go, my father says.

*

Boxes of books fill most of the living room. She's alphabetized them, which is very much like her. This way it'll be easier when you unpack them again, she says. They're never going to be unpacked, I say, I'm going to live an itinerant, rootless life, like a nomad, and furthermore, they were already organized by subject matter. But you just got an apartment, she says. I hope you haven't let my books touch any of your repugnant crime novels, I say. I think of my father. I bite my lip, trying to keep my words unspoken, but there's a little gap between two of my teeth and I can feel my lower lip slipping through. I take a deep breath. It doesn't work. I tell her what a shock my first edition of Thomasine Gyllembourg would experience if it ever stood alongside

The Da Vinci Code. The pages would practically start to crumble out, I scream. It's a wonder I have any books left at all after three and half years with you, I say, you've decimated my intellect. She asks if I want a glass of water. I ask if she wants some new books. Or if she'd rather just have a new girlfriend. Do you have to do this, she asks. As it happens, I'm in possession of a phone number belonging to a very sweet girl, I say. She's called Lis and she's a prison guard and she drives a Puch Maxi moped. Lis on her Puch, I say, sounds like a lesbian porno. She closes a box and says that this is a difficult situation for her too. That she still really cares about me. I ask her whether she's getting sentimental or if she's just been to another one of those non-violent communication workshops. She says I'm avoiding the issue. You make that sound like a bad thing, I say, you should think of it as a code, gaps requiring interpretation. Why do you always have to be so plot-fixated, I ask. I gasp for air. She asks if my asthma has been acting up lately. She sounds concerned. I say that I ought to donate my book collection to her in the hope that she might someday cultivate a proper literary sensibility, and to help her otherwise perfectly good bookshelves cope with the well-organized vulgarity she's furnished them with. Well, if you're planning on becoming a nomad then I guess I can take the books, she says. I know you, I say, you'd just sell them all to a drunken antiquarian for a scandalously low price, because you have no idea what real literature is. She closes another box. I open it back up. The box falls apart. A few books fall out. Look what you've done, I say. I point at her. And then you'd use all the money on a bunch of those awful books about the little boy who flies around on a broomstick and fights The Bad with The Good. I make giant quotation marks in the air. I ask if she's aware of my opinion on fantasy. She nods. No you're not, I say, because you never listen. You find the genre simplistic, she says, you think its basic values are aligned with the troubling rhetoric of the right wing, and that its unsubtle morality eliminates the complexity that is literature's greatest strength in relation to other artistic forms. As she speaks, she waves her arms and rolls her eyes and talks louder and faster, panting in an exaggerated Jutlandic accent. And furthermore, she says, jumping up onto a chair, the creation of magical parallel universes is inescapably problematic because they are inherently opposed to a real universe, which presupposes the existence of a real universe. She throws her arms up and gazes into the distance like a king surveying the masses. She cups her hands into a funnel and holds them up to her mouth. Is there such thing as reality, she yells, making giant quotations marks in the air when she comes to the word reality. I smile reluctantly. She hops down from her throne. I'm going to miss you, I say. You too, she says, it's been a lot of fun. I nod.

Monologues of a Seahorse VII

Behind my retina there is a photo album. I can't stop the pictures, they never cease, they continue in a long progression like a game of dominos in reverse, with pieces that don't fall down but rise up infinitely. You, sitting on the back patio, surrounded by flowerpots and succulents, the second before you notice my gaze from the window. A quick snapshot of your eyes as they meet mine beneath a streetlight and make me feel like the person I wish I'd been. Abstract paintings of your peculiar thought processes, childlike drawings of our plans for the future. A gold-framed photograph of you looking at your niece while I'm looking at you. The picture of your apple cores standing around the apartment like trophies, you always ate apples, little red apples, you always tasted like apples and smelled like apples, sometimes I almost thought you looked like an apple, were an apple. Six portions of fruit a day. You spoke of vitamin C and I thought of the fall from Eden. A charcoal drawing of my face, and I wonder if that was how you saw me or if it was just how you wished I looked. Half-finished sketches of wholehearted endeavors, hundreds of Kodak moments. A picture of you sleeping with a calmness that always astonished me, as if sacrificing yourself to something no one else dares believe in. Your profile in the dark as you sit at the windowsill and look into the night, and you with your soft cheeks, you always look like you've been out picking flowers, and I'm convinced that you're the most normal person I've ever met. Your wide eyes, and me noticing you noticing details, sensing your sense of beauty. A messy painting of the red splotches on your neck when you get angry, a fresco in a church, the music of a thousand organ pipes echoing through the room. The photograph of your naked body lying stretched on the kitchen floor late one night, half covered by shadows cast by swaying pots and pans hanging from the ceiling. And you with your eyes cast to the sky, you're a wandering abstraction, floating two and a half meters above the ground and speaking only of phenomena and things you cannot touch. A pencil drawing of you sitting in lotus pose on a rag rug and stretching your arms toward the sun in a state of fragile tranquility. The contours of your body behind the curtain in a changing room, the way you twirl in your dress and smile at yourself in the mirror, the tears you cried into the apple pie you never baked. A landscape painting of your childhood, a naive painting with hundreds of colors, this is the world as you see it. The photograph of you playing, a ray of sun hits your saxophone and lights it up and it looks like your arms are full of gold. A kite festival seen from the vantage point of the flat rooftop where you stand under a sky woven through with strands of white clouds and swarming with flying, swooping, dancing kites. I zoom in on the playful look in your eyes, the little shake you give your string as you watch your kite conquer the heavens. The elongated comic strips depicting us fighting as two-dimensional figures. I think of you as Daisy Duck, always offended by something or other. Your thought bubbles are empty, and in our speech bubbles there is only lightning and thunder and axes. And you with your obnoxiously inscrutable smiles that fill me with doubt, I want to paint your portrait and hang it up with a pushpin in the Louvre so Mona Lisa can take a break. And you sitting by the fireplace eating corn on the cob, surrounded by mountains of flatbread. Like a stern goddess you command and talk and yell and conduct the course of civilization with that corncob. A painting by a French impressionist, a mass of tiny dots that begin in your iris and turn into the pores in your skin, turn into your moles, turn into the little blonde hairs on your belly, your tiny broken blood vessels, your smallpox vaccination. When I come close, you're nothing more than flickering dots of many colors, and you only start to resemble a person when I'm so far away I can no longer touch you.

WE ALL HAVE a responsibility, my mother says on the phone. She wants me to come with her to solicit donations for The Danish Cancer Society. Of course we do, I say, I'm just really busy these days. I draw sketches of Kingo on a draft of a menu that my father's wife dropped off. Café Chrysillis, I write at the top in big looping letters. My mother asks what I'm so busy with. I talk a bit about my thesis, how I'm really getting into the flow of it. My mother asks if I've even found a research topic yet. I look down at my drawings. Kingo, I say, Kingo's role as an orator and the political influence of his hymns in the seventeenth century. I'm impressed by how plausible it sounds, and for a brief moment I consider starting to write a thesis. My mother says that if I'm so interested in the seventeenth century then I'd be better off writing about Leonora Christina, who was locked away in the Blue Tower. She wrote a whole book called The Memoirs of a Sufferer, my mother says, and she also whined constantly, it's just right for you. I'm sticking with Kingo, I say. My mother says that, regardless, I should be able to spare a few hours for collecting donations. No longer shall I be your Thrall, The Burdens you to me have yoked, These I cast from me, and do now refuse, I say. My mother says I should think about people other than myself. I think about Kingo, I say. He didn't have cancer, my mother says, he had it easy. He spent almost his entire life compiling a hymn book for the king, and then the whole thing was rejected because no one understood him, I say, that's what it's like to be ahead of your time. My mother says I should think about the world around me instead. What is all this, Which the World doth adorn with lovely forms, It is all but Shadows and glittering Glass, It is all but Bubbles, and echoes ringing through empty Vessels, I say. You've been brainwashed by your father, my mother says, it sounds like you've had some kind of religious awakening. She talks about how nice it would be to make a day trip out of it, to get some fresh air and do a good deed at the same time. Leisure Samaritans, I say, drawing a big smiling mouth on Kingo. I say that I don't want to be dispatched to some desolate corner of Aarhus to trudge around with a plastic bucket and beg innocent people for money as if it were Halloween. Are we going to start singing about cancer when they open the door, I say, or recite The Wretched of Odense Hospital. My mother says that we can choose our own route, and that it's always fun to see inside other peoples' homes. She talks back and forth with herself about how much you can find out about a family just from their entryway. You're pathologically nosy, I say. Sociologically interested, my mother says, it's part of my job. This is an opportunity to observe people up close. My mother keeps talking while I turn on my computer and search for my doctor's name. An address comes up on the screen near Marselisborg. Fine, I say, then let's take a route near the marina. My mother keeps trying to convince me how important it is until she realizes that I've said yes. My mother says I have no idea how relieved she is to hear that I've settled on Kingo. Time's ticking, my mother says. What are my Years, I say, which stealthily vanish and silently pass? What are my Worries? My Thought-filled Mind? My Sorrows? My Joys? The Spinning of mine Head? That's nice darling, my mother says, see you on Saturday.

*

My mother has brought a bottle of rosé in a bag. In her other hand she swings the donation bucket back and forth. We're going to be a big help to the sick today, my mother says. We sit down on a bench by the marina and my mother takes two thermoses out of the bag. Cheers for the cancer patients, she says, may they all get well soon. I light a cigarette. Screw it, my mother says, taking a cigarette from the pack, which she claims will be her one for the year. We look out at the marina, a seagull lands in front of the bench and watches us. It has a dead fish in its mouth. It's amazing that they can bring themselves to eat those things, my mother says. I tell her about my ex-girlfriend's family and their fondness for fish. Good thing you got away from those people, my mother says, it sounds morbid. My mother asks if I still miss her very much. I nod. Sweet girl, my mother says, no doubt about that, but she blended in with the wallpaper. She talked about animals all the time, my mother says, it was basically the only thing she ever talked about. I look out over the water. My mother takes my hand. Animals here and animals there and animals everywhere, my mother chants. She was a zookeeper after all, I say. My mother says that she doesn't talk about houses all the time just because she's a real-estate agent. I say that I just wish we could've been happy. Well you weren't, period, my mother says, you're dreaming of a fairy tale. But reality's an animal affair, I say. Are you quoting Shu-bi-dua, my mother asks. I nod. You're so lowbrow, darling, my mother says, good thing you've got Kingo now.

*

As we go from door to door the collection bucket gets heavier and heavier. When people don't answer my mother goes over to the window and looks in. If she sees anyone on the other side of the glass then she smiles and waves and points at the collection bucket. We're here to fight cancer, she shouts with a smile. My mother tells one young man that she herself has just recovered, so it's a mission that's close to her heart. She points at her right breast. Prosthetic, she whispers. This is unethical, I say when he goes to find some cash. People need personal stories, my mother whispers, terminal illness is incredibly hard to comprehend, it's so abstract. The young man comes back with two hundred kroner, and he invites us in for a cup of coffee. He asks if my mother still has any side effects from the treatment. You're never quite the same again, my mother says and points her at her, after you've looked death in the eye. The young man looks at her understandingly and nods. He tells us that his mother died of lung cancer four years ago. He turns to me and asks how I handled the situation. I clear my throat and look over at a photograph of a middle-aged woman on the windowsill. She was amazing, my mother says, darling, you were my rock throughout the whole thing. I nod. The man smiles at me and says that a strong support network is essential. I was lying there, my mother says, terrified and totally bald from the chemo, and my daughter came every day to cheer me up. She looks at me lovingly, and I get the impression that she's vividly remembering events that never took place. The man takes out a photo album and he lights up as he tells us about some of his childhood memories. My mother smiles and nods and asks him questions and the man looks happy. He gets another photo album and tells more stories about the woman in the pictures. It's important not to take your mother for granted while you've still got her, my mother says, looking at me. So true, you should remember that, the man says to me with a smile. When we go, my mother hugs the young man. He smiles as he shuts the door. I look at my mother when we go out of his garden gate. You're a raging mythomaniac, I say, as we drink the rest of the rosé. Nonsense, my mother says, I was exactly what he needed. My mother says that the truth is overrated. If you get caught up in the details then you'll die of boredom, she says, and that's almost worse than cancer.

*

We finally get to the last house on the street. My doctor's name is written on the mailbox. My mother rings the doorbell. Two shorts and one long. I straighten up a little and try to act surprised when my doctor opens the door. He looks at me, and I smile and hold out the collection bucket. My mother says that we're here for The Danish Cancer Society. My doctor stares at me. Wow, such a coincidence, I say, so this is where you live. My doctor nods. Small world, I say. It's not that small, my mother whispers when he goes in to get his wallet. My mother puts her heel in the doorway to keep the door from slamming shut. She pokes her head in. Very tasteful, she whispers, simple, but absolutely tasteful. My doctor's wife comes to the door and smiles. My mother praises the color of the walls and asks if that's a real Arne Jacobsen she sees there in the living room. I take a peek inside. There are teddy bears on the floor and hanging on the wall are some portraits of different children's faces. They're so cute, my mother says. My doctor comes back to the door and puts a hundred kroner in the bucket. He says he hopes we collect lots of money for the cause, and he smiles at me. I smile back and say I'll probably see him soon. I think I feel a sore throat coming on, I say, and I cough a little. It's probably just the cigarettes, my mother says. Can't you make her stop smoking, she says to my doctor. He says that sort of thing is a personal choice. I hope she's been on good behavior, my mother says, only children can be a little difficult. My doctor nods and shakes his head at the same time. You have a lovely daughter, he says. I certainly do, my mother says, she takes after me. He looks from me to my mother. We both smile at him. So she can't be all bad, my mother says, laughing loudly. My doctor smiles anxiously. You can forget all about that, my mother says after my doctor closes the door. I have no idea what you're talking about, I mumble. He's your doctor, she says, and he's married. Maybe she's just a flash in the pan, I say, like Kate. My mother concedes the possibility, and she says that his wife did blend in with the wallpaper. I nod. But sometimes I worry about your state of mind, my mother says, stroking my hair. I know, I say, I'd better book an appointment with my doctor. And furthermore, I thought you preferred women, my mother says. I say that she's the one getting caught up in the details, and that, furthermore, women have brought me nothing but trouble thus far. The bucket has gotten really heavy. There are going to be some happy cancer patients, my mother says with a smile.

*

The next day I go to the zoo. I watch her through the railings. She's training sea lions. I like seeing her when she doesn't know anyone's looking. She holds a ring out in the air and makes some strange noises. Two sea lions crawl through the ring. A third just stares at her, mystified. She throws two fish over to the sea lions that crawled through. The third one keeps staring. She laughs and brings the ring closer to it. It looks at the bucket of fish in her hand. She drops the ring and throws it a fish. When she catches sight of me she waves and smiles. We sit down under a tree. I say that the problem with our relationship was the way we communicated, that it was like we were talking past one another. She says I'm probably right. She asks if I want to get some ice cream and find a sunny bench to eat it on. It bothers me that she talks about food products when I talk about feelings. It feels like she's out of reach. Three sunbeams land on her face, the sun has always suited her. I say it was probably just bad timing. Timing is everything, I say. She points at my chocolate ice cream, which is dripping. My yellow pants are spotted with brown. You look like a giraffe, she says, laughing. Shit, I say. She hands me a napkin and says that we met at exactly the right time, that she wouldn't have had it otherwise. I eat the rest of my ice cream. You smell like happiness, I say, are you wearing Happy. She says that she is happy. Happy is a strong word, I say. She smiles and says I sound like my mother.

Monologues of a Seahorse VIII

Inside my nose there's a mausoleum, a gigantic Taj Mahal bearing the smells of the past. You with your skin that always smelled like spruce, you've ruined my Christmas Eves in perpetuity. And you with your clothes reeking of synthetic detergent, and not of flowers like you think. Your fingers that smell like sap, and your long hair that smells like cheap shampoo and blue King's cigarettes. Your shoulders smeared with sunblock and your skin covered in a thin layer of invisible salt water, everything about you smelling like summer. Clouds of smoke billowing up from a pan where chili and garlic and curry fry in oil as you emerge from the fog and smile apologetically. The smell of you when I step into your apartment, it can be neither fully articulated nor categorized, and I think of it as a mixture of old books, piles of paper, withered plants, and the thoughts you've jotted down. The heavy smell of poinsettias in your father's nursery, you standing in the middle of all that red. Your stubborn insistence upon citronella candles, scented candles generally, and your incense sticks in a clay pot at the bedside. The dirt on your hands, your sweat, your blood, the many fluid secretions of your bodies. Not to mention your skin at the borders between your shoulders and your throats, your deodorants, your moisturizers, your perfumes.

Miracle. Absolutely Irresistible. Desire Me, Chance, Pleasures, Obsession, Happy, Rush, True Love, Always Yours, Silenes, Cool Water, Contradiction, Realities. Poison, K.A.O.S., Nothing.

PART THREE

In which a milestone birthday approaches with a hurried gait, and our heroine sets off in search of winged words. We bid farewell to the doctor, who, for his part, speaks of chemical bonds and turns on the fairy lights at the end of the tunnel.

I LOOK DOWN at a menu written entirely in French. My mother and I are out at a restaurant. She takes a little notebook out of her bag and meticulously prints a line of tiny curlicues on a sheet of paper. She calls the waiter over and we order. My mother makes it clear with her body language that what she's writing is highly secretive. The waiter goes back to the kitchen with our orders. My mother whispers that she's doing it so the waiter will think that she's the food critic from a famous gastronomy publication. You're a real-estate agent, I whisper. My mother says that you've got come to reality's assistance when it doesn't suit your needs, and that she's doing it so we'll get better service and possibly a free sorbet. She smiles across the room at the waiter and studies the menu intensely. She says she needs to go outside to call her husband. The head editor, she says loudly in the direction of the kitchen while giving me a wink. The waiter nods tiredly. My mother has been here before. She dances out the door. I watch my mother through the window. She puts her glasses on and stares at her phone in concentration while typing a number. My mother always speaks loudly when she uses her cell phone, as if she doesn't entirely have faith in wireless communication. I can hear her voice faintly, but it's impossible to distinguish the words from one another. She takes a quick look around and finds a pack of Prince 100s in her bag. She lights a cigarette and smokes it while laughing into her phone. Then she cleans her hands with a wet wipe and takes a piece of chewing gum out of her pocket. The waiter walks in little circles with a bored expression. I order two glasses of white wine and pay for them at the same time. When my mother comes back into the restaurant she says that cell phones are an invention of the devil. So you resorted to smoke signals instead, I say. She chews her gum vigorously. The Indians were onto something, my mother says. She notices the wine and brightens up. It was on the house, I say. You see how it's done, my mother says. We raise our glasses.

*

I wake up in the middle of the afternoon when the doorbell rings. You lie beside me sleeping. I poke you ever so gently on the cheek to make sure you really exist. You open your eyes and smile. When I get to the door there's no one there. On the mat is a woven basket with a purple ribbon. A gigantic Easter egg sticks up out of the basket. The bottom of the basket is covered in differently colored caramels, and a stuffed yellow chicken stands guard over the egg. There's also a carton of yellow King's and five Easter beers. I gather from the card that this is a friendly greeting from the Easter Bunny. I see my father running down the stairs. Dad, I yell. It's the

Easter Bunny, he says in a high squeaky voice which echoes up the stairway. I grab the chicken by the neck and bring the basket inside. You look at me from the bedroom door. Why didn't your father come in, you ask. My father thinks he's the Easter Bunny, I say. You ask what I want to do today. I watch you as you take the caramels out of the basket and arrange them in little patterns on the floor. I'm going to divide myself into hundreds of pieces and assume the form of a harem, then I'll appear as sixteen immortal virgins, although it's a little late for that, and we'll surround you and feed you grapes and walk around you in circles with a fan in each of our thirty-two hands. I'm going to worship you like a rain god, tie you up to a totem pole and dance around you. I'm going to make an advertising campaign about you and hang your image in metro stations and trains and on the facades of houses, I'm going to unroll you like a poster and decorate the whole world, I'm going to loan you out to my best friends, and I'm going to make a silent film with you as the lead, it will be black and white with cheerful piano music as accompaniment. I'm going to take your picture while you're sleeping, or make a gardening show where you walk around in green spaces with a straw hat on and point at branches and talk about different kinds of trees. Or I'll make a documentary to inform the public about you, find home videos and film slides from your childhood, get your old classmates and distant relatives to share stories, and I'll carry you through the city like a golden trophy in my uplifted arms while I yell, just look at these dimples, I drink champagne out of them! You take a bite of a turquoise-colored Easter egg and look at me.

*

I tell my doctor that I'm feeling very strange, and perhaps it's because I've fallen in love. My doctor says that the sensation of falling in love shares many characteristics with psychological illness and drug addiction. I say that these comparisons could be perceived as insulting. What we know is this, he says, the thing we refer to as love is created in the VTA area at the bottom of the brain and in the caudate nucleus in the middle of the head. Both of these areas are important for the production of dopamine, which generates feelings of happiness. My skull is aglow with dopamine, I say. My doctor points out that the same chemicals are found in heroin, so there's reason to consider whether addiction is a factor. He says that we each have a general system for craving, and that the objects of our desire are interchangeable and irrelevant to the way the chemicals affect us. I think it's hard to manage all the emotions, I say. My doctor says that love has nothing to do with emotions. The VTA area and the caudate nucleus belong to the primitive part of the brain, therefore falling in love should actually be classified as an instinct. A sudden pedagogical impulse grips my doctor, and he grabs a notepad and a pen. He draws a circle, which I assume is meant to be the brain. I ask if it shouldn't be a little more elongated, it looks like a pizza, I say. He says he's a doctor and not an artist. He draws a heart a little ways away from the circle and makes some arrows pointing at the brain. He explains that love is merely a high concentration of dopamine in the brain combined with a low production of serotonin, which is the chemical that regulates our mood. The higher our serotonin levels, the happier we become, my doctor says with a cheerful expression. He draws a little square and writes serotonin inside it in block letters, and then he draws some more arrows pointing at a smiling face. My doctor tells me about an Italian researcher who demonstrated distinctive similarities between people who've fallen in love and people with obsessive-compulsive disorder. I take the pen out of his hand and draw a little man with a black mustache beside his drawing of the heart. I make a speech bubble where it says mamma mia and a dotted line over to the pizzabrain. He looks at my little Italian man and says that it was actually a female researcher. I add two braids, but I leave the mustache. Dark-haired women often have mustaches, I say. My doctor looks at the drawing and nods. He says that she measured the concentration of serotonin in the blood of a group of people in love and a group of people with OCD. Both groups had serotonin levels forty percent lower than normal. The overwhelming feelings of euphoria are combined with a kind of loss of self-control, my doctor says. He looks at me as if I've ceased to exist, and I can tell that my image has dissolved from his sight. He lectures on about test results while I draw a little seahorse inside the pizzabrain.

*

My mother calls and asks how things are going on the love front. I ask if it's necessary to use war metaphors. I can hear my mother walking around in her apartment in high heels. You're avoiding the issue, she says. You're clicking, I say. And have you clicked with anyone since I last saw you, my mother asks. She says that it's important to have clear ground rules so you know what you're getting into and you don't get hurt. I say that she's way too conceptual, that I won't be shackled by the chains of the petty bourgeoisie and put my emotions in a box just so that other people will be able to evaluate them. You should've been around in the seventies, my mother says, you'd have fit in so well, and back then we also wore shabby clothes. My mother says that she just wants to know if I've fallen in love with somebody, that a mother has a right to know these things. I say that people are born alone and die alone and they use the intervening time trying to convince themselves that there's a path out of this loneliness. That the concept of the romantic partner is an insane invention, that it's merely a synonym for escapism. You can't belong to anyone, I say. Don't be so philosophical, darling, my mother says, you'll just get depressed and have a hard life. Her heel clicks when she says hard. It's a long time since I've been this happy, I say. My mother says that she can easily make some changes to the seating arrangements should we have an extra guest at her birthday party. Kein Problem, she says, it's just a question of being creative. She says it's just wonderful that I've fallen in love. I hear her heel click when she says wonderful. Click, my mother's heel says.

Monologues of a Seahorse IX

Inside my knee there is a clicking metronome. There isn't much time between the clicks, they can come at a pause in a conversation, mid-sentence, after a silence, and the click cannot be explained or comprehended, it can only click. There are solitary clicks, repeating clicks, unexpected clicks, predictable clicks. It is your stilettos echoing through a tunnel, and it is the way you crack your fingers, and it is the sound of your hairclips clasping and of you putting the caps back on your tubes of red lipstick. I am a clicking bomb, and I'm on an endless quest for clicks in all their forms. I think of you, it is your eyes, your clicking glances. Sounds emit from your eyes, and they say click. It says click when your dimples appear and alter the form of your face. Click. It is the series of clicks when your fingers hit the keyboard, it is the click when you unlock the door, this metronome clicking within me is all of the sounds you make. When two people think of each other at the same time, a click echoes through the atmosphere. It is the sound of footsteps, the reverberations of a heartbeat, it is the bass line of a pop song, it is a rhythm you can dance to, it is a camera shutter, all these clicks that haunt me. It's a fireworks show of clicking sounds, these symphonies of clicks, it's the sound of the egg you crack into pieces one morning, it's the roulette wheel at a casino, the turn signal in a car. It's the latches of your old suitcase, it's a can of beer, backgammon. It goes click every time something important happens. When the second hand moves, when the pen clicks right before you sign your name, when an old cassette tape reaches its end, when an electric kettle turns off. Raindrops on rooftops, people clipping their nails, shifting gears, swordfights. It is the ticking of my biological clock, it is a lightbulb blowing out, it is the seatbelt I buckle, it is the car radio you turn on. It is when you close a lunchbox one early morning, when we eat rice with chopsticks at night. And I hunt them down, these clicks, they determine where I go, who I follow, flee from, run back to, catch up with, collide into, throw myself upon.

WHY DO WE always have to come to The Old Town, I say to Mulle, you're a living, breathing artifact. My spin doctor loves to wander The Old Town while thinking her deep thoughts. It's so quaint, Mulle says, can't you just feel the breath of history. You're so conservative, I say, people are walking around in costumes and pretending they were alive three hundred years ago, it's just weird. It's Denmark's answer to Disneyland, Mulle says, tugging me along. Let's go to the half-timbered house, Mulle says, Kingo was probably there back in his day, and you could use some inspiration. My spin doctor is excited, and she pulls me by the braid. It's like you're blind and I'm your guide dog, I yell. Mulle closes her eyes and waves her arms, c'mere Kingo, Kiiiingo. Woof woof, I bark, trying to bite her on the shoulder. A class of preschoolers walk by in two straight lines, forty-eight eyes staring up at us with curiosity. Good thing you didn't end up agreeing to have a baby, Mulle says. Two small boys straggle behind the group, they're in the midst of a swordfight and they stab at each other with broken branches. I think about Mulle and me when we were children, how we always zipped our matching pink jackets together when we went for walks with our preschool. You have to write me a speech for my mother's birthday, I say to Mulle, you're my spin doctor, it's your duty. What can we say about your mother, Mulle asks. She thinks I'm a whiner, I say. Mulle clears her throat and looks at me. But no more, I say, I've become a new and better person. Mulle nods and says that things were definitely worse last summer, now you only whine about Kingo, she says. Are you saying my mother is right, I ask. Your mother's always right, Mulle says, isn't that her motto. I nod. Then that will be our recurring motif, Mulle says, the throughline of the whole speech. We sit down at the Entré Café, Mulle takes a notebook and a pen out of her bag. Inventio, dispositio, elocutio, memoria, pronuntiatio, my spin doctor says. The throughline is that your mother is always right, you'll throw in some humorous confessions along the way, and finally, Mulle says with a clap of her hands, you'll say something touching. Tonal shifts make the funny more funny and the serious more serious, my spin doctor says. This isn't how you write a speech, I say. This is the only way to write a speech, Mulle says, if it were up to you then you'd just ramble on about seahorses and various abstract phenomena until everyone fell asleep. That's why humanists never amount to anything, Mulle says.

*

When I step into your apartment in the evening I walk right up to you. You have flour on your cheeks and two pizza doughs stretch themselves over the kitchen counter. Are we a couple, I ask you. You smile slightly and touch my hair. My mother says it's important to have clear ground rules, I say. You start slicing a salami and ask me what I think. I think we could partake in one another's neuroses, exchange compulsions, and stimulate each other's carnal appetites, I say. And we'll be poor but uncompromising artists and live in New York in a decrepit loft with no electricity. And we'll write incomprehensible poetry, metapoetic fragments with thousands of intertextual references to nonexistent Cuban philosophers, we'll scorn all ideologies and norms, and we'll win countless prizes so we can refuse to show up to the award ceremony because we just don't believe in that kind of thing. We'll critique our society and question the bourgeois lifestyle and we'll put sunglasses on the statue of The Little Mermaid in the summer and a balaclava on her when it snows while hundreds of Japanese tourists photograph us and we'll kiss passionately in this blitz of flashing lights, and we'll play harmonicas and live in the present and travel the world and establish true friendships with the locals and talk about how backpacking culture spoils authenticity and we'll problematize the concept of Danishness. You smile at me as you grate a block of parmesan cheese. And before we die, I say, we'll open a pizzeria, and we'll sleep in the brick oven beside the soft dough you'll have made in the first rays of dawn with an Italian recipe that's been passed down through generations. And our pizzas will be shaped like various punctuation marks and decorated with prosciutto di Parma and little bits of ground beef bound fast in the melted cheese, and our eyes will sparkle like two slices of pepperoni and we'll spontaneously break out in song as we live on the edge and make garlic marinades and sweep the kitchen floor and dance through clouds of flour. You say that sounds lovely.

*

It's May Day. Mulle and I are drinking beers on a blanket in the Botanical Garden. The sun is out, and Mulle is under the impression that she can play guitar. That's capitalism for you, she bellows, the poor are paid with scorn. Suddenly I see my ex-girlfriend walking through the trees with her binoculars. Mulle, look, I whisper, and I point at her. She's spying on us, Mulle says. I think she's actually bird-watching, I say. Mulle says that I should go talk to her. The power structure has shifted, my spin doctor says, now's your chance to seem balanced and thriving. Mulle has just handed in her thesis on political discourses. Furthermore, she has the right to know that she's been replaced, Mulle says, this will stabilize your relationship and allow you to communicate on an even footing. I walk slowly into the binoculars' field of view. She smiles and lowers her binoculars, then she hugs me and asks how I'm doing. I tell her that I have a new partner. And who is this lucky person, she asks. I'm just about to scold her for this blatantly sarcastic remark when I remember that she's never sarcastic. I say that I don't know if I'll ever figure out how to be a good girlfriend. You will, she says. I'm an only child, I say, we're really difficult. She says that she'll be sure to make a detailed instruction manual and send it to the concerned party. Can we be friends now, I say. Of course, she says. I don't mean just Facebook friends, I say, or people who send each other obligatory Christmas cards, I mean real friends like the ones Jodle Birge sings about. I get the idea, she says. I nod and say that I've quit being melodramatic and obnoxious. She says that sounds nice, but there's nothing wrong with having a healthy sense of drama. I say that it's like the leading lady walked off the set and I have to hire a replacement. It's like I suddenly forgot what play I'm acting in, I say. Don't you think you're just a little mixed up right now, she asks. Sometimes you're more precise than the most precise comparisons, I say, where'd you learn that. I must be uniquely receptive to reality, she says. When we'd just met each other you named a sea lion after me, I say, do you remember that. She says it was a very sweet sea lion, and she smiles at me. Let's buy heart-shaped friendship necklaces that say best friends, I say, do you remember those from the mid-nineties. That won't be necessary, she says, turning my face toward her own. You know me better than anyone, she says, you're just such a bad advertisement for yourself sometimes. I say that I'm sorry for all the things I said, and also for all the things I didn't say. I look at my hands. My lifeline is incredibly long, and my loveline cuts off in the middle. I show her the inside of my hand. She holds it between her hands and says that everything will work itself out.

Monologues of a Seahorse X

Inside my palm there is an art studio. I stand in the middle of the room with paintbrushes in my hair and paint splattered on my clothes, surrounded by massive canvases. The walls are hung with long rows of heroic portraits looking down on me, and I'm often reminded of your triumphant parades and your exploits. It is you who've been fighting in all my battles, and you've always been on my side. You are a guerilla army with green paint on your faces, lying in wait and defending me against my enemies. You are private chauffeurs in limousines when I've missed my last bus, you're a gang of proofreaders with eyeglasses on your foreheads who discover all my typos, and you're fat little Baroque angels with chubby cheeks who perch on my shoulders and whisper that I should do the right thing. You are all my keywords, you're my whole frame of reference, you're outstretched hands holding my asthma spray, you're the glow of lighters at a music venue where I'm singing, and you are patient prompters who whisper my lines when I get nervous, I catch your eyes through the little opening in the stage floor and suddenly I know just what to say. You are the natural boundary between me and my fears, the last stop before loneliness envelops me. You are the hands I reach for, you're a forest of open arms, you're open books and open eyes. It was you who brought about world peace, kneeling in your garage with peace signs in your eyes as you painted banners with big red letters, you were a stubborn goddess of chaos singing protest songs at Rådhuspladsen, and it was you who closed the hole in the ozone layer with a few brisk maneuvers, and then we never gave it another thought. And you who were my blue Mondays, you were fast-food restaurants and trips to the amusement park, a roller coaster screeching hysterically, you were the echo of all the world's laughter. And you who are a pizzeria I always want to go to, perhaps the little grimy one on Vestergade where the cheese stretches into meter-long strings between my lips and the pizza slice and it's you who are still open when I'm heading home one late night and my hangover hasn't yet defeated me, it's you who are number thirty-four with pepperoni and ground beef and bacon, and it's you I don't want to share with anyone. And it's you who are within reach. You are the panting, stabilized madness that coils within my body and slowly, quite slowly, assumes the form of an existence. I gaze up at your portraits for ten seconds whenever I feel a nervous breakdown coming on. It'll work out, you chant in unison, you're good enough, we believe in you, and I look back at this illustrious assembly and I know that you mean it. I know that there's nothing left to say, that the curtains have irrevocably dropped, that the rage has gone to rest and the longing has dwindled, that there are no more tears, and all that remains is a big, resounding thanks. Thank you for the time, thank you for the dance, thank you for the trust, thank you for the thoughts, thank you for the battle. Thank you for everything.

I'M AT MY father's house trying to write lyrics for my mother's birthday song. I hum fragments of various melodies. I Am the Oats, my father's wife says, it's a sure bet. Shine On You Crazy Diamond, my father says, Pink Floyd, you can't go wrong. You can't write lyrics to that, I say. My father looks hurt, and he walks over to his wife's piano. Pink Floyd is coming to play in Denmark, my father says. He tells me that my mother claims to have had an affair with David Gilmour when she was young. My mother is a compulsive liar, I say to my father. I tell him about our outing collecting money for The Danish Cancer Society. He smiles. I can't imagine how she got custody of me as a child, I say, she's so unreliable. Your mother may be a bit nuts, my father says, but one is never bored in her company. I ask why he always has to defend her, aren't you supposed to hate your ex-wife, I say. My father's wife nods. I tug at my hair and look down at the paper. My mother calls and asks where I am. In a cellar dark as coal, I sing, way down deep. My mother asks if I've made the invitations for her birthday party. I say that I've scanned her baby picture for the front page, but that I haven't written the lyrics yet. She says that my father and I are the absolute slowest people she knows. Mom says we're slow, I say to my father. Thorough, he mutters. Your asthma's acting up today, my mother says, I can hear it in your breathing. It's the pollen, I say. It's the cigarettes, my mother says. I groan. I received eighteen years of child tax benefits in exchange for relaying that kind of information, my mother says. What rhymes with irritating, I say to my father once we've hung up. Fascinating, he says, remember that it's a birthday song.

*

Mulle's grandmother rolls around in her wheelchair speaking her mind. She has a gigantic straw hat on with a big plastic flower reaching for the heavens. I've received eleven compliments today, people say I match, Mulle's grandmother says. Mulle tells me that they've been to bingo at the Senior Club. Mulle's grandmother asks if I also think she matches. I say that her leopard-print blouse complements her pleated turquoise skirt in a most eye-catching manner. She nods in satisfaction. You smell like garlic, Mulle's grandmother says, have you eaten something ethnic. Mulle's grandmother tells us about some Muslims living in her building. They play strange music, she says, and they procreate like rats, every morning there's another little pitch-black child down in the courtyard. It's all right for people to be different, Mulle says, the world's a global village nowadays, we're not in the nineteen-thirties anymore. But we're close, Mulle's grandmother says, looking over at The Old Town blissfully. There weren't any of those turbaned ladies around back then, and there aren't many here either, she yells. She is very bad for your political career, I say to Mulle. My spin doctor asks how my speech for my mother's birthday party is coming along. I'm a bit stuck, I say. That sounds like you, Mulle says. My mother says I was fat when I was little, I say, is that true. You were a very portly little girl, Mulle's grandmother says, you had these big fat cheeks, they looked like balloons. I look down and see her leopard-printed arms pointing at my stomach. And whenever it was windy out your upper arms would flap in the breeze, Mulle's grandmother says, just like jello. Remember that you're not allowed to hit old ladies, Mulle says. Mulle's grandmother looks up at her. And your mother's completely bats, she says to Mulle as she puts on a pair of big sunglasses. Mulle's mother was admitted to the Risskov psychiatric ward several times during her childhood, so she spent long periods living with her grandmother. Mulle looks down at the grass. My mother's batty too, I say, putting my arm around Mulle. Half of Mulle's grandmother's face is now covered by dark sunglasses with thick gold frames. You look like Michael Jackson, I tell Mulle's grandmother. He was such a phony, Mulle's grandmother hisses, always jumping around like a brute. And that nose that was always about to fall off, Mulle's grandmother says, once black, always black, but at least he tried to look like us. My phone rings, it's my father. Hey little lady, he says. Is Grethe sick again, I say. Is it the priest, Mulle's grandmother whispers, straightening her hat. My father is in Fona. I'm fourth in line, he says breathlessly. It's Pink Floyd, my father says.

I say that I've been trying to get tickets online all morning but it didn't work out. My father has transformed the parsonage into the headquarters for the hunt for tickets, and today's the big day. There's a map of Denmark spread across the table and he's enlisted people in various regions of the country to wait in line outside their local music stores and to try to get through on the phone. You've been planning this campaign for a month, I say, what could go wrong. I have a funeral at two o'clock, my father says, and the ticket website is down, you've got to get over here and take my spot in line. My father sounds desperate.

*

Mulle and I run behind the wheelchair. What about the concert on the promenade, Mulle's grandmother yells, what's wrong with you people. We're helping the priest, Mulle says to her grandmother, he wants to go to a concert. Well so do I, Mulle's grandmother seethes. The wheelchair is really heavy. Perhaps you're the portly one, I say to Mulle's grandmother as we race along the canal. You're just out of shape, she says, conducting us through the city. By the time we get to Fona the line reaches all the way to Clemens Bridge. We park Mulle's grandmother outside and find my father. He looks worried. It's incredible how people always seem to die at the most inconvenient times, I say. We'll never get tickets, my father says. He's sixteenth in line now. You're no good at pushing and elbowing, I say, you've been letting people get in front of you, you're just too sweet. My father looks sad. They haven't played The Wall since the wall fell, he says morosely. He checks the time and kisses Mulle and me on the cheek before running out to the car where his wife awaits him with his gown. There's a sudden tumult at the back of the store. The line divides in two as people move to the side, forming a little alley up to the register. My mother marches down it with a triumphant smile, pushing Mulle's grandmother in front of her in the wheelchair. I hear fragments of my mother's voice. It has an appealingly familiar ring to it. She's saying something about Mulle's grandmother's terminal diagnosis and how she wants to see Pink Floyd one last time before she passes on. It's my dying wish, Mulle's grandmother yells. Half a year left at most, my mother says. She talks about ending life in style. People let them by instinctively and shout for others to clear the way. How I long to hear Pink Flute, Mulle's grandmother screams. Now I hear that Mulle's grandfather apparently died around the time that the wall came down, and that the music of Pink Floyd reminds Mulle's grandmother of their life together. She's taken her sunglasses off, she clasps her hands and smiles faintly. My mother strides through the crowd. When they finally reach the front of the line, my mother turns around and thanks everyone for their touching generosity. You've made an old lady very happy, my mother says. People clap and smile.

*

It's evening and you're reading in my bed. I look at my computer screen. I have a document open called thesis, but unfortunately it's blank. You leaf through the newspaper, your dark curls fall down over your forehead, and you push them back again and again with your fingers, almost automatically. You ask how it's going with Kingo. You look very serious, even when you smile, as if you're keeping all the world's secrets. I imagine an ancient Chinese garden inside of you where pink cherry trees bloom and people sit in white-painted tea houses, confiding in one another. My body's full of fireworks, and I ready myself for a declaration of love. Suddenly I can't remember how you're supposed to say this sort of thing. I suppose it should be spoken somewhat seriously, perhaps by moonlight. It's getting dark out and the moon is almost full. I can see it sitting atop the cathedral like a glowing cupola. I clear my throat and embark into a long monologue. You look shocked, and you ask if I'm about to break up with you. I freeze and say no, no, this is going great. I think maybe I should say it in the midst of a burst of laughter instead, so there can be no misunderstandings, love is a happy thing after all. It should be one morning when you're in your narrative mood, telling one of your countless stories, and just as your laughter is cresting, at the second when I think I probably had to be there, right in the brief soundwave when our laughter blends together, that's when I'll say it. But then it might come off as unserious, I think, not sufficiently profound. There must be some middle ground, a mix of the happy and the serious, maybe on a perfectly normal day. I could say it totally casually one evening while we're making dinner: Not so much chili pepper, pass me the coconut milk, I love you, do you think it needs more salt, I said no more chili pepper for god's sake, I really do, the spaghetti's boiling over, could you take the lid off, I've wanted to say it for a long time, no, all the way off, I really mean it, I love you. But this, on the other hand, might be too mundane and insignificant. I could also go for simplicity, just stop you in a doorway, take your hand, and say it. But what if you were to back up and say: Whoa, that was intense, have you been drinking, or: Don't you think you're taking this relationship a little too seriously. Or maybe you'd smile and say that's so sweet and then quickly change the subject to an article you read recently about sewage contamination, or say you needed to pop down to the store for some cigarettes and never come back. Or what if you just repeated my words with the greatest of ease, almost without a pause, like you thought I said it just so you'd have to say it too, and, rather than considering whether the statement was true, you said it back to avoid an awkward situation or to spare my feelings, which is of course considerate, but also boundlessly humiliating. I clear my throat and say that there's something I'm finding very difficult to say. You put down your book and meet my gaze. You have letters in your eyes and ink on your fingers. She sells seashells, I say, it's almost impossible. You nod slowly. Especially if you say it over and over again, I say, it's doomed to fail. She shells sea hells, I say, you might as well not even try. You start talking about the importance of making an outline and you point to my desk. This is really uncomfortable for me, why do you have to be so literal, I say. We chat about bibliographies and primary sources. I drift off to sleep while we're discussing the finer points of my argumentation, but you stay at my computer and look through my books. I hear you sifting through literary history and talking to yourself. When you finally lie down beside me I can feel your synthetic soccer jersey, probably the blue one that says Pelé. You brush my hair away from my ear and lie close beside me. She sells seashells, you whisper right before I fall asleep.

Monologues of a Seahorse XI

Inside my throat there is a cathedral, and it is here that the words are hidden. There's a ribbon tied around my vocal cords, but I'll find them, the words I'm always searching for. I love you, I whispered one night when I was sixteen, still unsure as to whether it was just a thought. But the walls cast their sound back, and my words sounded like thunder until you repeated them. And suddenly it became more real because the thought turned sound and became this sentence that was vibrating in a brief, neon-colored now. You who sat on the lawn under the chestnut tree with your guitar, bells ringing in your braids, you wanted to change the world, and I expect you're still trying. That's why there are holes in every guitar in the world, you said, the resonance, the air is where the sound is amplified. They apply to every one of you, these three words, those of you who'll always return to me and those who I only knew a short while, you who I watched slowly disappear, and you who were gone in an instant. They are caught in my throat, and they ring out in this cathedral, the three words, they are toys and surprises and chocolate, they are the holy trinity of our faith. Three small words gathered into a sentence, sounds that tie people together inextricably, they are beginnings and endings and long boring passages, they are the preface, the story, and the epilogue, the first wavering note, the last fading echo, they are free jazz and a chorus from a pop song with endless key changes, the world's shortest symphony, they are an enormous gospel choir in a cathedral singing their joy out into world.

MULLE AND I have hangovers and we're watching a romantic comedy on my bed. I say that just like everyone has different names, every name should have a unique declaration of love with a special meaning associated with it. That way the previous ones could keep shining bright, I say, and remain true within their own time periods. You humanists have so many problems, Mulle groans. And each new declaration of love would be its own truth and not some reverberation from the past, an echo of all the faces tied to those same words. I say that I don't know how to say I love you anymore. Mulle says I should just imagine that I'm an alcoholic at my first AA meeting. You've just got to say it out loud, Mulle says, that's how you come to terms with it, and the next time it'll be easier. What if there's just an awkward silence after I've said it, I say. Mulle nods and takes off her glasses. She says that a declaration of love is one of the most power-structuring statements there is. In one way it's a kind of surrender, she says, but it also forces the respondent into the position of an involuntarily receiver, so in that way you would maintain your power with respect to the established roles. I nod and light a cigarette. My spin doctor suggests that I pretend I'm saying it in my sleep. Mulle lies down on my bed with closed eyes. I love you, she whispers half-intelligibly then starts snoring. She sits up again and looks at me. If there's no response, she says, then you can toss around a little and act like you're just dreaming. Maybe I could say it in another language, I say. Or sing it, Mulle says, like Whitney Houston in The Bodyguard. You watch so many bad movies, I say. Mulle says that I'm the one she watches them with, which means that I do too. When I watch bad movies it's called camp, I say, my relationship with popular culture is exclusively one of critical observation. The doorbell rings.

*

Outside the door is my mother's husband. My mother asked him to stop by and fix the drain in my kitchen. Mulle and I debate which language is best suited to declarations of love. Albanian, my mother's husband says, *te dua*. Te dua, that's so bland, Mulle says, te dua, it sounds like a slogan for a bank. Agreed, I say, it should be a bit more expressive. Cambodian, the voice under the sink suggests, *soro lahn nhee ah*. That sounds more like a sigh or a yawn, Mulle says, it won't do, she'd only be able to say it at night. *Bahibik*, my mother's husband says as he hammers on a pipe, it's Lebanese. Very rhythmic, it has a nice swing to it, Mulle says, drumming her fingers on the kitchen sink, it sounds almost like a beating heart. She puts her hand on my heart. Ba-hi-bik, ba-hi-bik, she chants. Too festive, I say, it sounds like something you'd yell when you were saying cheers or happy new year, it doesn't seem lofty enough. My mother's husband pokes his head out from my kitchen cabinet and looks at me despairingly. There are little drops of water in his gray hair. Gaelic, he says, *ta gra agam ort*. Mulle shakes her head, it sounds like you're casting a spell, she says. I nod. Witch's brew and elixir of love, wing of bat and butterfly bones, spider's blood and just a little sprinkle of ta gra agam ort. It won't do, I say. My mother's husband gets up and turns on the faucet and looks down at the pipes. He nods in satisfaction. I find three beers in the refrigerator. Bahibik and thank you, I say. Half a case of beer later we've arrived at Mandarin Chinese. *Wo ai ni*, my mother's husband says. It sounds too much like a nursery rhyme, I say. Mulle says she thinks it was one of the practice exercises back in elementary school, when we were learning to write our vowels in cursive. We sit in silence. *Negligevapse*, my mother's husband yells suddenly, negligevapse. Sounds nice and relaxed, Mulle says, almost joyful. Five syllables, three different vowels, nine different letters, plenty of anagrammatical possibilities, I say. Negligevapse is just one word, Mulle says, it totally transcends the power structure by eliminating the giver-receiver relationship. What language is it, I ask. It's Inuit, my mother's husband says. Is that spoken by the sinusitis peoples, I ask. Sinusitis is an infection in one or more of the paranasal sinuses, my mother's husband says. Children with recurring sinusitis often have Kartagener's syndrome, my mother's husband says, which can also cause situs inversus, commonly known as reversed organs. Negligevapse negligevapse, Mulle sings.

*

Negligevapse, I whisper in your ear the next morning. You open your eyes for a short second and smile before falling back to sleep. I call Mulle and tell her that it seems to be the exact right word. When you get up a few hours later, you say you feel like you've got a head full of moss. Big soft tufts of moss, you say as you stretch. You say that when late summer comes around you're going to hike all the way to Funen, just wander in your own thoughts and take photos of blades of grass and poppy flowers until you get there. You'll have an old blue baby carriage that you'll push in front of you all the way. Can I sit in the baby carriage, I say. Maybe, you say. Negligevapse, I say. All right, all right, you say, whatever you say. I try on the dress I'm going to wear to my mother's birthday party. You run the fabric through your fingers and marvel that you managed to capture such a perfect human specimen in the wild. Negligevapse, I say, looking away. Don't say that, it looks lovely on you, you say. I hang it up again and think about my speech. You make the coffee and I'll go get the cinnamon buns, I say, teamwork is teamwork. I hum all the way to the baker. Negligevapse, I sing, it always fits. When you've beaten me at dice for the sixth time at the pub and can no longer conceal your triumphant smile, I'll hold out my hands in resignation and moan negligevapse, and you'll say I know you are but what am I, and it's just a game, and when we pedal through the morning traffic and you say that I'm biking like a psychopath and beg me to buy a helmet, I'll look into your worried eyes and whiz through a red light and turn back and yell out negligevapse so loud that all Tordenskjoldsgade trembles, and you'll say you didn't mean it like that, that you'd just like to hold on to me for few more years. I'll say a slightly distressed negligevapse when you scream at the television screen and hammer your clenched fist down on the table. Negligevapse, I'll say forgivingly, and you'll say it's out of the question when Contador is such a cheater, and that cycling isn't the sport it used to be. Other times I'll mumble it ever so softly and you'll look up from your book, half-lovingly and half-enraged at the interruption. We go shopping, we go roller skating, we drink coffee at laundromats, we play guessing games on the bus, we make sand sculptures on the beach, we kiss in intersections and rent movies and build little towers of french fries at fast food restaurants. Negligevapse, I say. One afternoon when you're a bit bored you'll look up negligevapse in your copy of the New Danish Dictionary, then you'll check your etymological lexicon, but no answers will be forthcoming. An annoyed wrinkle will appear on your forehead, you'll scratch your chin and call your father and ask him to look it up in his dictionary. You father will be thrilled at the opportunity to sing the praises of the dictionary and he'll also quickly point out various shortcomings of modern technology. You'll close your eyes halfway and take a deep breath and say ne-gli-ge-vap-se. Your father will start flipping through the pages, and you'll be able to hear them crinkling through the telephone, and he'll put his glasses on and turn the pages faster and faster. The annoyed wrinkle on your face will make its way across the Lillebælt Bridge and run right into your father's forehead, and he'll scratch his chin and say there must be something wrong with the word because the dictionary works perfectly well. You'll be very stubborn and refuse to ask me what negligevapse means, and you'll draw little diagrams and graphs detailing how frequent and in which situations I say negligevapse. And you'll sit up all through the night with your colored pencils and try to decipher a pattern, but you'll slowly lose interest and start to suspect that it's just a sound I make compulsively, perhaps a fragment of a song I'm misremembering, and you won't know that it's a recurring declaration of love. In the end you'll start to say it yourself, just for fun at first, imitating me the way you do when you think I'm being ridiculous, but after a while you'll start to say it regularly, because we'll have gradually adopted each other's turns of phrase and expressions, and maybe then we can just tell each other negligevapse whenever it pops into our heads.

*

It's been a while, my doctor says when I walk through the door. I say that I'm a ticking bomb of dopamine, that I might explode at any minute. My doctor says I seem happy. I look at my doctor's wedding ring and ask him if he believes in everlasting love. He says that what comes closest is devotion, because it's produced in the areas of the brain that are controlled by our emotions as opposed to our primal instincts. And what causes devotion, I ask. As our dopamine production decreases along with the constant feelings of euphoria it inspires, it is replaced by the hormone oxytocin, my doctor says. Isn't that also a stain remover, I say, stains rejected, colors protected. He shakes his head and says that it's a hormone produced in the pituitary gland, which hangs on a stem in the middle of the skull. So love is just dangling on a hook in the middle of our skulls, I say, that seems worrisome. Actually, I'm ecstatic. It's a little bell that rings, it's a bat sleeping upside down on a telephone wire, it's the skeleton of a dead fly swaying in a spiderweb. It's a raindrop on a clothesline, it's a tear on an eyelash, it's a summer hat on a coat rack. In any case, my doctor says, oxytocin increases the sensitivity in our nerves and causes muscular cells to draw closer together. So an arbitrary muscle contraction determines our ability to form lasting bonds with another person, I say. Or animal, my doctor adds, field mice become lifelong couples because they produce extremely large quantities of oxytocin, it's what enables us to enter into monogamous relationships. I don't know if I'm capable of forming lasting bonds with anyone, I say, how do you know if it will work out. Similarly, a high oxytocin level in both parties of the relationship helps ensure that the two people will stay together, my doctor says as he fidgets with his wedding ring. So the people who generate our dopamine aren't necessarily the same ones who'll stimulate our oxytocin, I say. He shakes his head apologetically. But maybe once every hundred years they merge into one, I say. He tells me about a study that found that one in ten couples can, after many years together, still produce the same brain chemicals as people who've just fallen in love. In the romantic partnerships that last, both parties fall in love following the same mental pattern as swans, he says. Never say always, I say, nothing is certain. Only science, my doctor says, and he tells me about research that was done on a number of happily wedded couples who'd all been together for over twenty years. When these couples saw photos of their spouses, their fMRI scans revealed quantities of pleasure-producing dopamine which are usually only exhibited during the very first phase of a love relationship. Is this conclusive evidence that love is real, I ask. My doctor nods and smiles and assures me that no one can cheat on a brain scan.

*

My mother will turn sixty on Saturday. We're at her cottage in Amtoft making flower arrangements for the tables. A mountain of pink and white roses rises in front of me. My mother is happy, and she laughs up into the sunlight. She waves her arms and talks about how much fun it's going to be. Her flower arrangement is haphazard and the little plastic figure in the middle resembling my mother is about to fall off. Where did you find these things, I say, you look great in plastic. My mother says that they were originally made for wedding cakes, but she sawed the grooms off. Down in the trash can I see eight lonely plastic men. This time it's *my* big day, she says, laughing. My mother asks if I've written a song for her. A speech would also suffice, she says, since you're spending so much time on your thesis these days. My mother looks at me sympathetically. You'll whip it out in no time, darling, you've always been so interested in language, she says. She goes into the kitchen and comes back and hands me a list of keywords that she wrote. I know how busy you are, she says. I look down at the paper. It's just a helpful guideline, my mother says, you don't have to use it, but I do think you should include the bit about the dog. I look at the paper again. The highlights of her life are bullet-pointed in chronological order. You were only three in nineteen fifty-four, I say, I wasn't even born yet. I've told you that story a bunch of times, my mother says, about the time I found the lucky almond in my Christmas pudding. I nod. My mother starts telling me about the time she got the lucky almond. She had four sisters and they lived on a farm in Himmerland. She'd spent the first three years of her life dreaming about winning the lucky almond at Christmas dinner. I affix my mother to the center of bunch of roses with a clump of clay. Well, I always had to share everything with my sisters, my mother says, so the thought of having the lucky almond all to myself was the most wonderful thing I could imagine. Yes, I think you've mentioned that before, I say. My mother tells me how she found the lucky almond. And I got it fair and square, darling, not the way your father does it, always putting the almond in your bowl. That kind of privilege is reserved for only children, my mother says. I nod. The prize was a box of chocolates, my mother says, which your grandmother had bought, and this was right after the war, so there wasn't much money around. Nine years after the war, I say. Anyway, I was such a generous little girl, my mother says. So you shared your chocolates with the whole family, but when you were done the box was empty, and there were none left for you, I say. That's exactly right, my mother says with a smile, you remember it like you were there yourself. Can't Aunt Lise give that speech, I say, it might seem more authentic. My mother says that I'm being difficult, that she's only trying to help me, and that, furthermore, she thinks this particular story perfectly captures her personality. I look down at her bullet points, it says North Jutland's Sunshine Girl of the Year, 1970. I think I've heard something about you cheating in that competition, I ask, that's what Aunt Bente says. Nonsense, she's just jealous, my mother says, I don't remember any cheating. Remembering is a creative process that builds on one's ability to recreate situations, I say, what can seem like a factual event is actually a construction of the mind. That's what I told your aunt Bente, but you know how she is when she gets an idea stuck in her head, my mother says. I look at her note for the year I was born. That's when I had you, my mother says, that was the best day of my life. I can't get up at your birthday and tell everyone that I'm the best thing that's ever happened in your life, I say. Don't be so modest, my mother says, that won't get you anywhere in this world. I read through the rest of her bullet points, and I see that they continue on the other side. There's enough here for a whole book, I say. That's a distinct possibility, my mother says.

Monologues of a Seahorse XII

My skin is covered in a chaos of invisible paintings. One morning I wondered what I would look like if your hands left traces, if from your fingers there flowed stripes or dotted lines, little points forming patterns over my body. I imagine that everyone who's ever touched me exists not as a number or a name or a memory, but a color. I think how my body would become a brilliant painting, how I'd be a wandering rainbow of intimacies, an acrylic painting of touches. I imagine that I'm a graffiti-covered tunnel, that each of you are inside this tunnel with a can of spray paint in your hands, leaving your signatures on my walls. I wonder whether I, too, am tramping around inside of other people, whether a cosmic exchange of intimacy exists. Your fingers hit the keys, gently, skin meeting ivory, and music streams into the room. We both shook so much the first time that our teeth collided. Every part of us crashed together in this unaccustomed intensity. My hand shook on your neck, but your neck was shaking too, and it was impossible to tell which movements led to which. I feel you like a phantom limb, the sum of your forgiveness and the weight of your resignation washing over my body, as images of toppled card houses, crumbling ruins, and collapsed castles in the air run through my mind. I imagine that you are tattoos, that you've burrowed under my skin, elongated, chaotic tattoos wrapping around my body. And I carry your memories and pasts and childhoods, because within my seahorse there are hundreds of other seahorses, and I drag your accumulated anguish and your bursts of laughter behind me with every single step I take.

HUNTER SIMPSON is originally from North Carolina and lives in Copenhagen, Denmark. Stine Pilgaard's *The Land of Short Sentences* (World Editions, 2022) was his first published literary translation and won the Scandinavian American Foundation's Leif and Inger Sjöberg Prize for 2021. *My Mother Says* is his second published translation.

Book Club Discussion Guides are available on our website.

By the same author:
The Land of Short Sentences

World Editions promotes voices from around the globe by publishing books from many different countries and languages in English translation. Through our work, we aim to enhance dialogue between cultures, foster new connections, and open doors which may otherwise have remained closed.

Also available from World Editions:

The Leash and the Ball
Rodaan Al Galidi
Translated by Jonathan Reeder
"Al Galidi has an eye for the absurd."
—*Irish Times*

Cocoon
Zhang Yueran
Translated by Jeremy Tiang
"A remarkable and tragic story."
—*Publishers Weekly*

Tale of the Dreamer's Son
Preeta Samarasan
"Samarasan's inventive prose is stunning."
—*The Guardian*

Abyss
Pilar Quintana
Translated by Lisa Dillman
"Small details that can define an entire continent."
—*Vogue*

The Gospel According to the New World
Maryse Condé
Translated by Richard Philcox
"Condé has a gift for storytelling."
—*New York Times Book Review*

On the Design

As book design is an integral part of the reading experience, we would like to acknowledge the work of those who shaped the form in which the story is housed.

Tessa van der Waals (Netherlands) is responsible for the cover design, cover typography, and art direction of all World Editions books. She works in the internationally renowned tradition of Dutch Design. Her bright and powerful visual aesthetic maintains a harmony between image and typography, and captures the unique atmosphere of each book. She works closely with internationally celebrated photographers, artists, and letter designers. Her work has frequently been awarded prizes for Best Dutch Book Design.

The drawings on the cover are by renowned Dutch illustrator Annemarie van Haeringen, based on objects featured in the story. The title font is Bodega Sans Old Style by Greg Thompson. Released in 1990, Bodega Sans adopts numerous ideas from the high period of Art Deco, providing designs that are as fresh as they are nostalgic. This geometric series, along with its later serifed companion, is unique in offering both angular and rounded forms of each weight.

The cover has been edited by lithographer Bert van der Horst of BFC Graphics (Netherlands).

Euan Monaghan (United Kingdom) is responsible for the typography and careful interior book design.

The text on the inside covers and the press quotes are set in Circular, designed by Laurenz Brunner (Switzerland) and published by Swiss type foundry Lineto.

All World Editions books are set in the typeface Dolly, specifically designed for book typography. Dolly creates a warm page image perfect for an enjoyable reading experience. This typeface is designed by Underware, a European collective formed by Bas Jacobs (Netherlands), Akiem Helmling (Germany), and Sami Kortemäki (Finland). Underware are also the creators of the World Editions logo, which meets the design requirement that "a strong shape can always be drawn with a toe in the sand."